HOLIDAY SUMMER

by

DECIE MERWIN

THE CHILDREN'S PRESS
LONDON AND GLASGOW

First printed in this edition 1966

For I. V. A. Dundas

PRINTED AND MADE IN GREAT BRITAIN

CONTENTS

1. Leaving London

MARY LEE WADE stood on the platform in the cold grey light of Paddington Station and stared at a huge pile of luggage. How could four people—three really, for her father would be returning to London after establishing the family at the farm—how could three people, then, need so much? But a farm—an English farm, in April—meant extra clothes—rubber boots, raincoats, woollen mufflers. And, without doubt, boredom.

London in April was exciting, delightful with lush, well-kept parks, each with its lake or stream, their banks a golden glory of daffodils. Tall trees showed the first promise of spring, flower-carts made a splash of colour at every corner and there were gay window-boxes wherever one looked.

It had been fun just riding through the crowded, curving streets on the upper deck of a big, red bus. Dad had shown her Buckingham Palace, where the Queen lived, and Westminster Abbey. Twice they'd watched the changing of the guard at Whitehall.

Mary Lee had put it all down in her diary, the pretty little blue book with a metal clasp, which her favourite teacher had given her. Miss Logan had said that she must write up her experiences each day, that it would "stimulate her interest in both history and literature." What would there be to write about on a farm with every day exactly like the one before?

She hated to leave London. They hadn't meant to, either. They'd hoped to find a small flat and make it their headquarters for the summer while her father carried on the work he'd come all the way from Virginia to do.

Mary Lee's brown gaze came to rest on her young brother who was sitting disconsolately on the largest suitcase. It was Pat's fault—this sudden change of plan, this move to the country. Why did he have to get influenza a month before their sailing date? Why did he have to be seasick all the way over? She hadn't been seasick. She'd enjoyed every moment of the crossing and come ashore at Southampton ten short days ago with heightened colour and a ravenous appetite.

Pat looked up, caught her glance, and gave her a little fleeting grin.

For a moment Mary Lee hated herself. He looked so little and so forlorn. He seemed to have grown smaller since his illness. Surely his overcoat was a size too big now. His eyes were enormous in his pinched white face and there were smudgy circles under them. Like a lost kitten, Mary Lee thought, and she remembered guiltily that Pat had been shut up in a hotel bedroom all the time she was having a grand fling around the city with Dad. Mother, too. Even when Mary Lee had offered to stay—and she had offered, she remembered with satisfaction—Mom had been unwilling to go out. There was always some reason. Pat's temperature must be watched; the doctor might be coming. Then, after several days of steady improvement, Dr. Baker had recommended the country. Lots of fresh air, he said; build the boy up with milk, butter, eggs; long nights of sleep and a rest every afternoon. A comfortable farm would be the ideal place, preferably in one of the south-western counties; the climate was a bit milder there.

Searching through advertisements in newspapers and periodicals, the Wades had located a farm. Questions had been asked and answered; final arrangements made by telephone.

Mary Lee's mind went back to that particular ad., as she stood by the pile of luggage.

"Country living," it read. "Paying guests accommodated. Own farm produce. Transportation and riding available. Children welcome." The address followed. "Mrs. Randall, Somerhaze, Midsomer-St. Mary, near Bridgwater, Somerset."

Well, it was nice to know that Pat would be welcome. Pat was only eight. Of course, as she'd pointed out to her parents, she herself was far from being a child, since she'd passed her thirteenth birthday. She'd felt a mild interest in the words "transportation and riding available." A car would mean that they might escape for a little while when her father came down for week-ends. And Mary Lee loved riding. At least, she had loved it last summer when she'd taken a few riding lessons at a stable near home. This would be very different, of course—round and round a field on an old plough-horse probably.

"There's Dad! And a porter! Our train must be ready." Mrs. Wade's tired face brightened as she spoke.

The next few minutes were busy enough getting through the gate, down the long platform, on to the little hissing train, finding an empty compartment. The heavier luggage would go "in the van," the porter told them; he would see to it all. The smaller things were stowed in the racks overhead, and Mary Lee sank into a window seat with Pat facing her.

"Such a funny little train," Pat observed, tucking one foot under him to make himself comfortable. "But I like it. It's a toy train."

It did seem almost a toy when one remembered the great stream-lined train in which they had travelled from Virginia to New York, but Mary Lee noticed that, after a single shrill squeak from the little engine, they slid smoothly out of the station exactly on time.

The streets, the factories, the suburbs with their rows of dingy houses, each with its own small garden where forsythia and daffodils made a brave showing in spite of grime, were soon left behind and a country landscape lay beyond the window. Great cloud shadows made an ever-changing light and a winding river, full to the brim, curved its quiet way through fields half-green, half-golden with dandelions where sheep and cattle grazed.

"Lovely! Oh, lovely!" breathed Mrs. Wade, her eyes following a man in a battered old hat and well-worn tweed jacket, two shaggy dogs at heel, walking slowly across one of the flowery fields. "It's all so gentle, isn't it? That river is the Thames, I suppose?"

Mr. Wade had been in England before. The rest of the family expected him to know everything about the country.

"Yes," he answered now. "Our unit was stationed not far above here—nearer Oxford."

Pat had his small nose almost against the glass. "It's—it's a very—historical—sort of river, isn't it, Dad?"

His father looked surprised.

"It sure is, son. People speak of it as 'liquid history.' We can't be very far from the meadows of Runnymede where King John signed the Magna Carta and you can't find anything more 'historical' than that. But I hardly thought you'd have heard of it—yet."

"I haven't," Pat said indifferently. "What I meant was, I think it's the river where Moley went to live with Water Rat. And Mr. Toad, when he was pretending to be a washerwoman, ran off with the Barge people's horse. Don't you believe it's that river, Mom?"

Mary Lee burst into laughter.

"Mother's been reading *The Wind in the Willows* to him, Dad," she explained, when she could control the last of her giggles. "It's as true as history to Pat." Then, seeing the puzzled expression on her brother's face, she added quickly, "I'm sure it's the very river, Pat Those trees along the bank are willows, all right, and if you watch carefully, you might get a glimpse of Toad Hall. It had lawns sloping down to the water, you remember, and a boathouse."

"'Onion-sauce! Onion-sauce!'" Pat quoted his favourite character, Mole. After that, so long as the river remained in view, his attention never left the window.

There was too much difference in their ages for the brother and sister to be very companionable. Living in a small university town—a university at which her father taught—Mary Lee's every effort was bent on growing up as quickly as possible. Pat was, from her point of view, hopelessly young, though she often found him amusing. Watching his eager little face as his eyes searched the landscape for Toad Hall, she realised how much she'd missed his high spirits lately; it was good, she thought, to see Pat waking up at last.

2. *Train Journey*

THOUGH she still regretted leaving London, Mary Lee found the train journey fun.

There was so much to look at; and all so different from home. The villages they passed seemed tiny—cottages of stone or mellow brick for the most part, usually clustered about a square-towered church, old worn walls everywhere, pastures divided by hedges and groups of trees, and always with a glint of water reflecting the light. Even the larger towns were compact, appearing suddenly out of the fields, ending abruptly in fields again. There were farms a-plenty, looking like even tinier villages with their many barns and out-buildings. The stone which formed their walls grew rosier as the train moved westward.

The Wades had the compartment to themselves until lunchtime. When they returned from the restaurant car, however, they found one of the seats occupied by a pleasant-faced, middle-aged woman. She was unconcernedly eating a sandwich and a small lidded basket stood on the floor close to her sturdy brown shoes. Infant cat-sounds emerged from it.

The window ceased to be interesting. Neither Pat nor Mary Lee had eyes for anything but that basket.

"A kitten," the woman said, with a friendly smile. "For one of my grandchildren. Take him out if you like. The guard won't mind, unless you let him run into the corridor. Do you go far?"

"To Bridgwater," Mr. Wade told her, while Mary Lee carefully removed a yellow kitten from the basket. "We're to be met there and driven on to a place called Midsomer-St. Mary. I wonder if you know it, by any chance?"

"Oh, yes," was the reply. "A charming village, quite small, and well off the main road. Thatched cottages and a duck pond. Rather a good little church—fourteenth century, I believe. It lies just under the Quantock Hills and that part of the country is unspoilt. Or was. I haven't been there for years. Are you making a long stay?"

"We—we don't quite know." Mrs. Wade hesitated as she spoke. "Several weeks probably, if the place suits us. We have accommodation at a farm called Somerhaze. I don't suppose you remember it?"

"But I do!" their companion exclaimed with enthusiasm. "The house itself is something of a gem—Tudor—Elizabethan, I'd say, not later. The same family has lived there for generations. Now what was their name? . . . "

"Randall," Mary Lee supplied quickly. "Oh, do tell us about them!"

She knew her father would begin inquiring about the house, if given half a chance Houses were his interest and delight—the older, the better. He had come to England to explore old houses and write a book about what he called their "influence on early colonial architecture." But Mary Lee wanted to hear all she could of the Randalls because people, she thought, mattered more than houses, especially if you were going to live with them. So . . .

"What are they like?" she urged. "The Randalls."

"Oh, very pleasant, as I remember," the lady said. "I met Mrs. Randall now and then in the lane and once she asked me in for a cup of tea. There was a boy—a nice lad—who came down and played with our children. He'd be grown up long since, probably married and with children of his own, if the war spared him." She sighed. "Circumstances must have changed a lot for that family if they're taking paying guests. But it's good to hear that the house hasn't changed hands. Randalls belong there—including the family ghost."

Mary Lee stared with wide eyes.

"Don't look like that, my dear. You aren't afraid of ghosts, I'm sure."

"N-n-no, but . . ."

Mary Lee wondered if she was being teased.

"Our old families cherish their ghosts, you know. And this one will never bother you, for she only appears to gentlemen; that was the story around the village, anyway."

She turned then to Mrs. Wade.

"Somerhaze will do your boy a world of good," she said. "He looks peaky. And you'll enjoy it, too. You're the sort of Americans—oh, yes, I knew you for Americans at once—to appreciate the house. *Not* a showplace—but so lovely. One of those E-shaped houses with really beautiful mullioned windows. . . ."

Mary Lee sighed and stopped listening. She knew by the expression on her father's face that the conversation would deal with houses from here on. And it did. They became so interested that there was quite a flurry getting the lady off the train at Bath, and the kitten, which had been sleeping peacefully in the warm crook of Pat's arm, was almost overlooked and had to be thrust hurriedly through the corridor window in the last split second before the train pulled out.

"I wish she'd left it," Pat murmured sleepily. "It was a good little cat."

"Cheer up, son," his mother advised him. "There are sure to be cats on a farm. And where there are cats there are kittens—inevitably. You had a nap as well as the kitten, didn't you? But you'd better stay awake now. It can't be far to Bridgwater."

Mr. Wade, who had been trying to see as much of Bath as was possible from the window of a moving train, slid back into his seat and pulled a map-book out of his pocket.

"Not far," he announced. "Bath is in Somerset, I know. What a town! I must spend several days here soon. You might come with me, Mary Lee."

Mary Lee was flattered. She loved going about with her father. But her mother's comment had a sobering effect.

"Mary Lee," she said, "has got a lot of studying to do. Her school wasn't at all happy about her leaving in the middle of term, you remember. I promised faithfully that she would keep up with her work. Pat's illness has made things difficult. Oh, dear, I'm afraid neither of the children has opened a school-book for three weeks or more!"

"Oh, but I'm going to," Mary Lee gasped. "I'll begin to-morrow! I'll begin to-night!"

Her mother smiled. "I hardly think that will be necessary, darling. But you and I must settle down to regular hours soon. I'm rusty, I know, but I'll try to remember enough from my short teaching career to help. It might even be fun. We can take turns for some little trips with Dad later. There's so much over here that will make history come alive for all of us."

With this Mary Lee had to be content for the time being.

Her father was assembling the luggage.

Mary Lee stood up and shook out her grey flannel skirt, then peered into the small square mirror that was sandwiched between pictures of West Country beauty spots above the seats. She was frankly pleased with what she saw there. Of course she would never have the sleek, angular good looks of the models she so much admired in *Vogue*—not even when she grew up. Her face was too round for that. But the cool damp English air had brought colour to her cheeks and a deeper coral to her mouth. The soft brown hair which waved reluctantly at home now curled forward prettily under her grey felt hat.

She gave a final tug to her hat, retied the bright scarf at her throat and smiled a trifle wistfully at the vivid reflection in the glass. A pity, she thought—yes, rather a pity—to waste it all on a farm.

3. *Somerhaze*

MARY LEE had formed a clear mental picture of Mrs. Randall. She was elderly, white-haired, comfortably stout. She wore a knitted cardigan against the chill of an English spring, over a blue cotton dress, and a big checked apron. There was a basket of eggs on her arm. Of course she would not bring eggs to the Bridgwater station, nor the apron, but both remained stubbornly in the picture.

Nothing could have been more different than the young woman who came forward to greet them as they stepped from the train. Tall, she was, and slender. And almost smart, in a well-fitted brown tweed suit, pigskin gloves and polished, low-heeled country shoes. A blue silk scarf tied over smooth chestnut hair, matched the blue of her eyes.

She held out her hand, saying in the prettiest possible voice, "It's so nice to see you. I'm glad the train wasn't late; we'll be home in good time for tea."

"But—but——" stammered Mrs. Wade, and Mary Lee realised that her mother was as much surprised as she. "Are *you* Mrs. Randall? You're so *young*! I felt sure, when we talked on the phone, you were a much older person."

"Oh, you talked to Mother; my mother-in-law, that is," the young woman explained quickly. "There are two of us, you see. I'm Rosemary Randall; Mrs. Mark, they call me in the village."

Then her eye fell on the pile of luggage, growing more impressive every minute as boxes and suitcases were handed down from the van.

"Oh, dear!" she said. "Oh, dear. However will we get all that in the car!"

And, when they saw the car, the Wades wondered, too. It was old; it was battered. It was built to take four people in some degree of comfort, five at a pinch. And what, indeed, about the luggage?

"Isn't there a taxi?" asked Mr. Wade.

"But it's nearly fifteen miles," protested Mrs. Randall. "It would be so expensive! No, I can take all of you in the Biscuit Tin," She paused to laugh and explain. "That's what we call the car.

It rattles like a half-empty biscuit tin, but it does get you there. Your things could come to-morrow by carrier. Or the bus people are very obliging; perhaps, if I talked to them, they'd fetch it out this evening."

"If there's a bus," interrupted Mrs. Wade, "and it stops anywhere near the house, why don't we take it ourselves?"

"Oh, would you mind?" Mrs. Randall smiled at this suggestion. "It's a big green bus marked 'Minehead,' and it will be along in about ten minutes. Ask the man to put you out at the Heart-in-Hand—that's the pub—and then it's only a short walk down the lane to the farm. You can't miss it. I wonder if the little boy—Patrick, is it?—would like to come with me. He looks a bit . . ."

"Don't tell me. I know," Pat said irritably, but, before his mother could reprove him, he looked up through his lashes and saw Mrs. Randall's smile.

"I—I look 'peaky,'" he admitted in a small voice.

"Well, you won't look that way for long, once we get you to Somerhaze," she assured him. "And now, are you coming with me, or not?"

"Yes," answered Pat promptly, "I am."

He climbed into the front seat of the old car and waited contentedly there while the luggage was piled in the back.

"That," remarked Mrs. Wade, watching the

Biscuit Tin nose its way out of the station yard, "must be an example of the 'bracing' attitude I've heard the English employ with children. I'll admit it worked. I've never seen Pat take to a stranger so quickly."

Mr. Wade laughed. "I don't blame him," he said. "If the rest of the Randalls are at all like her, we're in luck."

When the bus came, Mary Lee was glad to find it a double-decker, and promptly suggested that they go on top. Even so, they caught only glimpses of the gardens behind high stone walls on either side of the road on the long climb out of Bridgwater. But when they reached the crest they saw a glorious expanse of country, more rolling than any they'd seen from the train. In the hazy blue distance the warm purple Quantock Hills shouldered the sky.

Thick hedges had taken the place of walls, and these were starred with pale yellow flowers at the base—primroses, Mary Lee supposed—and frosted white on top with what her father told her was blackthorn blossom.

Once, the bus stopped in the narrow road to let a herd of red and white cows saunter past. The man who drove them touched his shabby hat, whistled an order to his dog, and called, "Thank you, Ed," to the bus driver.

"Cattle's always got the right of way," was the good-natured response. "Heard the cuckoo yet, Tom?"

"Not yet. 'E's a bit late this year, 'ent 'e?"

The bus moved on. Did the driver know everyone along the way, Mary Lee wondered? The conductor, too. Whenever a passenger alighted at village or crossroads, he had a friendly word to say as he handed down a basket or parcel.

Mr. Wade twisted and turned in his seat, trying to see from both sides of the bus at once.

"It's the cottages," he confessed, laughing at his own enthusiasm. "I don't want to miss one. For sheer charm, the thatched cottage has never been surpassed."

Mary Lee agreed with him. "The roofs come right down over their ears," she said, "and the windows are like tiny bright eyes peeping out."

Mrs. Wade sat quiet, her hands folded in her lap.

"Tired, Mom?" Mary Lee asked.

"A little. I've been thinking about to-morrow."

"The unpacking, you mean? I'll help you with it. If you'll let me I could do it all."

"Oh, it wasn't that," her mother said, smiling. "I was thinking that to-morrow, if Pat is all right, I'll go out and pick the biggest bunch of primroses anyone has ever seen."

It was a long ride to Midsomer-St. Mary, a short walk down the lane to the farm.

They passed through the village which was, indeed, a charming one. A small clear stream paralleled the road. Sometimes this was spanned by short bridges leading to garden gates and eventually it gurgled its way into a pond where great trees were reflected in still water, and four snow-white ducks sunned themselves on a stone coping.

Here an even narrower lane turned off and the word "Somerhaze" faced them on a wooden farm gate standing hospitably open.

Pat came pelting down a rough drive to meet them.

"Hallo!" he shouted, as if he hadn't seen his family for a week. "I'm to shut the gate after you so the calves won't get out. There are three baby calves and some older ones in a field. I've been all over the barnyard and seen the pigs and hens and everything!"

"Oh, Pat," his mother said, a little worried. "I'd hoped you'd rest until we got here."

"I wasn't tired," Pat told her. "And Rose said . . ."

"Rose!"

"She said I could call her Rose." Pat was, for a moment, quelled. "Because two Mrs. Randalls are sort of mixing—and Rose is such a pretty name. Aren't we going in, Mom? Mrs. Randall is getting tea and I'm hungry."

They were standing outside another gate, a rusty, wrought-iron one set between stone posts, in an old stone wall. Immediately behind it stood the house.

Mary Lee never quite got over her first impression: that human hands had had nothing to do with building the house. It had grown there, like the ivy and Virginia creeper that covered so much of its walls, and seemed to hold it low on the ground for there was only one step up to the arched doorway. Afternoon sun glinted in small-paned, stone-shafted windows and warmed the whole house to a rosy glow.

"And to think," said her mother, "that we just picked this place out of half-a-dozen ads. in a newspaper!" Then she turned practical. "If only," she added, "if only the food is possible, and we don't freeze to death. Shall we go in? I see someone waiting at the door."

The "someone" was the elder Mrs. Randall. And again, Mary Lee's mental picture was wrong. The white hair was right, and she was wearing an apron, but it was a tiny crisp affair with ruffles, which set off a soft woollen dress. A small woman, quick and bird-like.

"I'm so sorry," she said as she shook hands, "that you had to take the bus. Are you cold? I'm afraid our old houses always seem chilly to Americans, but there's a good fire in the sitting-room. Rose will take you upstairs, and tea will be ready as soon as you come down." She turned to Mrs. Wade. "I thought Pat might have an egg and a glass of milk—some buttered toast, perhaps, instead of scones. You'll want to get him to bed early. Nothing like plenty of sleep for a child who's looking not quite the thing."

"So," muttered Pat to his sister a moment later on the stairs. "So I've got to go to bed early . . . Well, she didn't say I looked 'peaky' anyway. Perhaps—just for that—I will."

And, since he stumbled on the top step, Mary Lee thought it was a good idea.

4. *Enter Gillian*

MARY LEE wakened early next morning. For a drowsy moment she wondered where she was.

A cow called; a calf answered; she heard the clank of a metal bucket; a man's voice and the sound of boots on stone. A scent of wood smoke sweetened the chilly air.

She was at Somerhaze Farm!

But there had been another sound, surely; one that blurred with a dream—a dream of the bus and a farmer driving cattle.

Cuckoo! Cuckoo! Cuckoo!

The bus driver had asked the farmer if he'd heard it yet and the answer had been, " Not yet. 'E's a bit late this year."

Then she, Mary Lee Wade, must be listening to the very first cuckoo of spring!

Of course she'd never heard a cuckoo before but she'd read of such a bird and this one sounded so like a cuckoo clock she knew she couldn't be mistaken.

Cuckoo! Cuckoo! The cry was fainter now.

Nevertheless, Mary Lee slipped out of bed and padded, barefooted, to the window. Its narrow leaded casements opened outwards on either side of a stone shaft. Doves fluttered about a paved yard and strutted on the red-tiled roofs of barns that surrounded it on three sides. She could see no other bird and oh, the air was cold!

She pulled the casements shut and leaped back into her warm bed where she lay looking around the little room. She'd been too tired and sleepy last night to notice more than the strangeness of great dark beams that reached up the cream-coloured plaster walls to the ceiling, meeting other crossbeams there. Now she saw how low that ceiling was. The door, too. Dad would certainly have to duck his head to enter it. The old-fashioned furniture was almost as dark as the beams, but the big pitcher and bowl on the wash-stand were decorated with pink roses; pink curtains matched the counterpane on her bed, and there was a bowl of fresh violets on the chest of drawers. A delightful room, really; Mary Lee liked it.

Was that a knock at the door she had heard? Mary Lee called "Come in," and a girl entered, a small tray in her hands.

Mary Lee, surprised, could only stare, and for a moment, the girl stared back from grey-blue eyes that tilted ever so slightly at the corners. Her short, pale gold hair looked wind-tossed and her face was faintly pink all over. She was oddly dressed. A white cotton, coat-like garment to the knees was unbuttoned and showed a yellow turtle-necked sweater and much-faded jodhpurs underneath. Despite the absurd costume, the girl reminded Mary Lee of a very young and boyish angel she'd seen in one of the stained-glass windows at Westminster Abbey.

But the vision spoke in words that had grown familiar since coming to England.

"I've brought your tea, and it's a lovely morning."

The tray was set down on a little table beside the bed. Steam rose invitingly from a brown pot and there were three thin slices of bread and butter.

Mary Lee was hungry, but she continued to stare at the girl.

"Do—do you live here?" she asked at last.

"Oh, yes, I'm Gillian. Gillian Randall. Shall I pour your tea for you? And do you like one lump of sugar or two?"

"One, please—and a lot of milk."

Mary Lee sat up, huddled her woollen dressing-gown around her shoulders and reached for the cup.

The girl turned towards the door.

"Don't go away!" begged Mary Lee quickly. "Not until I've asked you a few questions. I can't think why Mom didn't find out more when she phoned down here. Is Rose—I'm sorry to call her Rose but I've caught it from Pat—is Mrs. Mark your mother? She looks awfully young to have a daughter as old as you. You weren't at tea or supper last night and nobody said a word about you."

"I can't explain everything at once," Gillian said, perching on the foot of Mary Lee's bed. "I mustn't stop because Mummy needs me, but why don't you come down and have breakfast with us in the kitchen? It's warm there. And your mother and father aren't to be called until eight-thirty. It's just on seven now. I heard you close your window when I let the dogs out, so we knew you were awake and Gran said I'd better bring you your tea."

"Dogs? I didn't see any dogs last night."

"No. They were with Jeff and me at Cary Court. We had supper there because Mummy thought you'd want a quiet first evening. She said that meeting so many new people all at once might not be good for your little brother who's been ill. I hope he wasn't too tired last night," she ended politely.

"No. He was full of pep. Who's Jeff?"

"Jeff is *my* brother. He's older than I am—I'm twelve. Mummy married when she was only eighteen, which is why she seems so young now—to be our mother, I mean."

Mary Lee opened her mouth for another question, but Gillian picked up the tray in a business-like manner.

"We can't stay nattering here," she said, "or breakfast will be ready before you are. I'll meet you in the dining-room in fifteen minutes. There are a lot of passages and things between it and the kitchen. You'd quite likely get lost."

She was gone.

For just a minute Mary Lee sat hugging her knees. A girl! An attractive girl near her own age! She saw life at Somerhaze in a new light—and it was anything but dull.

Ten minutes later she was dressed and downstairs.

Dad had had what she called a fit over both dining-room and sitting-room last night. Of course it was a quiet fit, but she'd known he was wildly enthusiastic about the oak panelled walls and plastered ceilings. The ceiling in the sitting-room had a delicate moulded design of grape-vines, with leaves and curling tendrils. And there was a high, lovely window, too. Mary Lee would have known it was a beautiful room, without Dad's raving. But the dining-room was dark, with a wider, shallower window on only one side. It had been very dim last night with the cherry-red curtains drawn and only candles on the table. She hadn't even noticed the big picture at the far end of the room.

She stood in front of it now, her hands clasped behind her back.

The face was Gillian's: the colouring, the tilted eyes, the arched brows. But the pale-gold hair was arranged in elaborate curls and the mouth curved in a sweet, mischievous smile—a come-hither smile, Mary Lee thought. The girl in the portrait was older than Gillian—grown-up—a bride, perhaps? She wore a very low-cut dress of what looked like ivory satin with great puffed sleeves and a long billowing skirt. The fingers of one slim hand touched the jewelled necklace around her throat, the other caressed the head of a fawn-coloured greyhound reared against her knee.

"That's Chloe." It was Gillian's voice behind her. Mary Lee had been so absorbed she'd not heard her enter the room. "I—I'm supposed to look like her—rather."

"You do," Mary Lee said, turning round. "Exactly," she added, studying Gillian's face which grew even pinker under her scrutiny. "Did she live here once?"

"Yes. Charles I's reign, it was. She brought this house into the Randall family. She was a Cary and her father gave her Somerhaze for a wedding present; I think they called it a dowry then. Anyway, it was when she married our great-great—

I don't know how many greats—grandfather. Breakfast now. . . ."

They went through a long narrow passage and a scullery. Both were stone floored and Mary Lee could feel the cold underfoot through the heavy brogues she was wearing.

It was delightful to enter the warm bright kitchen where a coal and wood fire burned in a big black iron stove set into what might once have been a fireplace. There was still a mantelpiece above. It held a row of painted canisters and several brass candlesticks.

Though the room was a large one, rugs on the floor and two or three wooden arm-chairs made it seem cosy.

A grey cat sat beside a bowl of primroses in the yellow-curtained window, washing her immaculate white bib with an equally white paw.

Rose was ladling hot porridge into blue bowls and Mrs. Randall poured boiling water from the kettle to the teapot.

"I love your kitchen, Mrs. Randall!" Mary Lee said.

"Do you, child? An English farm kitchen must seem strange to you, after the wonderful modern ones in the States. I often marvel at pictures of them in American magazines. Everything electrified! We have a small electric stove now—it's good for hotting up things or boiling a kettle—but the current is dear. Expensive," she explained, seeing Mary Lee's puzzled expression.

"And since we need the old stove for warmth, we might as well cook with it. The barns are wired, of course, because of the milking. I sometimes think our cows live in greater luxury than we do." She laughed and changed the subject. "I hope you slept well. Did you hear the cuckoo this morning? He was the first one this year."

Mary Lee nodded.

"I looked out but I couldn't see him," she said.

"One seldom does. He's a shy rascal."

And conceited, probably, Mary Lee thought. Why shouldn't he be with everyone talking about him? Then she turned her attention to the delicious fried bread and bacon on her plate.

Breakfast over, Gillian began stacking the dishes on a trolley.

"You needn't bother with them this morning, darling," her mother told her. "It's Mrs. Buffin's day for the roughs and she can wash up at the same time. Perhaps Mary Lee would like to have a look at the ponies."

"Oh, I would!" Mary Lee saw Gillian's face light up. But she wheeled the trolley into the scullery and shoved a few carrots into the pockets of her white coat before the two girls stepped out of doors.

They were greeted at once by the spaniels, one black, one golden.

"Fun and Frolic," Gillian introduced them.

"Down, dogs! Don't let them jump up on you, Mary Lee. They know better, and their paws are muddy."

"Oh, but they're sweet!" Mary Lee was fondling a head of each.

"You like animals, don't you?"

"Love 'em!" was the reply.

"Well, it seems a bit silly, staying on a farm, if you don't. That's the cow barn." Gillian waved a hand towards a long low structure with an open shed supported by great round pillars along one side. "We milk about twenty-five cows. Ayrshires. Except Venus and Diana—they're Jerseys."

Mary Lee would have loitered in the farmyard for she thought it picturesque. Dad would like it, she knew. All the buildings, of the same stone as the house, looked as if they'd been there forever. Lichen and moss clung to walls and roofs and a flight of worn steps leading up to a loft.

They followed a rough cart-track beyond the barns which soon brought them to the paddock gate.

Gillian lifted the latch and went through.

"There they are, the lovelies!" she exclaimed. "In the far corner, under the oaks. You can sit on the fence while I lure 'em over."

She gave a whistle and a grey mare raised her head, ears cocked, then started towards them, stepping daintily over the lush grass, still wet with dew. She was followed by two brown ponies and a cobby blue roan.

Gillian divided her carrots evenly.

"Here," she said. "You feed old Mousie and one of the ponies—their names are Bramble and Skittles—and I'll tend to the others."

She touched her cheek to the mare's soft muzzle and smiled at Mary Lee, her eyes shining.

"My Posy," she murmured. "Rather a darling, isn't she?"

"Oh, she's beautiful!" Mary Lee agreed wholeheartedly. "Do you ride her?"

"Yes, sometimes. She was foaled here; Mousie is her mother. But I ride the ponies mostly right now because we're boarding them for some people over at Stogary. When their children come home for the summer holidays they'll want the ponies in prime condition and easy to handle."

"I see." Mary Lee, reminded of school, wondered how Gillian happened to be free on a weekday. Easter vacation, of course!

"How long do you have at Easter?" she asked.

"A month. It's just begun."

"A month! We only have ten days."

"But I've heard that American schools break up early in the summer," Gillian said. "June, isn't it? After this holiday we go back until late July. It evens up, I dare say." Her attention returned to the horses. "You know, Mary Lee, if you ride, we can take the ponies out together. Fun—don't you think?"

Mary Lee looked doubtfully at Bramble as he flattened his ears and nipped at Skittles. Skittles gave a little squeal and wheeled around.

"Here, you two, no kicking! Be off!" Gillian ordered, giving one of them a sharp slap. He shied away from her, indulged in a mild buck, and galloped across the field, followed by the other horses.

The dogs pursued them, barking wildly, until Gillian whistled them back.

Mary Lee laughed, suddenly remembering how she'd pictured herself on an old plough horse. There'd be plenty to put in her blue diary if she rode one of these ponies!

"Honestly, Gillian," she said, "I don't know if I could manage that Skittles or not. I'm game to try, but I've only had a few riding lessons."

"Riding lessons," echoed Gillian. "I've never had any lessons but I've ridden all my life. I wouldn't put you up on Skittles anyway, not at first. Bramble is a quieter pony. And both of them want a bit of schooling. Jeff and I might give them a work-out this afternoon."

Jeff! Mary Lee had forgotten about Gillian's brother.

"Where is he?" she asked. "Your brother, I mean."

"He's staying at Ivy Cottage with Nannie Chilcott. Nannie gets offended if she can't have Jeff for a few days now and then. She used to be our nurse; our father's nurse before us. My father," Gillian went on, seeing Mary Lee about to ask another question, "my father was killed in the war, before I was born. I'm a posthumous child."

Mary Lee had no idea what "posthumous" meant but she suddenly felt she was being too curious. Her mother wouldn't approve at all. Perhaps Gillian didn't either.

Mom and Dad would be up by now. They'd probably finished breakfast. And she couldn't wait to tell them all about her early morning adventures.

"I promised Mom I'd help her unpack our things," she told Gillian.

"And I must make the beds for Mummy," Gillian said.

The two girls walked briskly back towards the house.

5. *Enter Jeffrey*

THEY MET Pat in the yard, on his way to visit the pigs.

He said "How-do-you-do" very nicely to Gillian. Pat's manners were at their best this morning; all was right with his world.

"Has Mom started unpacking yet?" Mary Lee asked.

"No, and I wouldn't say anything about it, if I were you. The minute she sees our books she'll begin talking about lessons again; you know how important she thinks school is. There's so much to do around here. I won't have time for lessons for ages."

Pat continued on his way to the sties.

Mary Lee eventually found her mother in the garden.

The house faced south and the garden, except for a flagstone walk, filled the shallow space between it and the wall There was the iron gate through which the Wades had entered yesterday, and, at the end of the walk, another one, set in a crumbling stone archway, pointed at the top like a church window.

"Mrs. Randall told me that arch leads to a rose garden," Mrs. Wade said. "I peeped through. The roses don't bloom until June here, but, oh, my dear, look at these!" She held up a double handful of valley lillies and little blue Scillas. "And the cherry and crab-apple are in full bloom. I've taken some branches of those indoors. They're utterly lovely!"

"But, Mom, did you know about Gillian? Did you know she has a brother, Jeff? I had breakfast in the kitchen because I woke up early, and then Gillian took me out to see the horses. She says I can ride with her! You'll let me, won't you, Mom?"

"Of course, dear, if you'll promise to be careful. Yes, I heard you had breakfast with the family. And Mrs. Mark told us about her children last night after you'd gone to bed. They'll be pleasant company for you and Pat, I imagine."

"Mother," Mary Lee spoke softly, seriously. "What's a posthumous child? Gillian said she was one. Does it matter?"

"Matter? Of course not. It only means that she was born after her father died."

"Oh," Mary Lee breathed a sigh of relief. "I —I thought it might be some sort of disease. And I didn't like to ask in case it was."

Her mother burst into laughter.

Mary Lee suddenly realised how well she looked—how rested. And she was gay once more, the way she used to be before Pat's illness.

But her mother's face grew serious again. "One thing, honey," she said, "while we're on the subject of Gillian. She probably helps her mother and grandmother a good deal. You'll be careful not to take her away from her tasks, won't you?"

"Yes. Maybe—maybe I could help with some of them?"

"Perhaps both of us can be helpful," her mother agreed. "But we must go about it slowly, daughter. English people are reserved, you know. I wouldn't want the Randalls to think that we were interfering. It's sad that Mrs. Mark should have lost her husband so young. She's very brave, it seems to me. Mrs. Randall, too. I imagine she was used to a much easier life than she has now. But they're both so cheerful, and determined to keep this place going until Jeffrey has finished his education and can take on the farming. Luckily he's enthusiastic about it—or so his mother says."

Mrs. Wade gathered up her flowers. "I really ought to go and unpack."

"Let me do it, Mom. After all I said I would."

"Would you, Mary Lee? Just your things and Pat's. Where is Pat, by the way? Have you seen him?"

"Yes. I met him in the barnyard. He's crazy about the pigs."

"He seems to be," Mrs. Wade agreed, smiling. "But he looks wonderfully well this morning, doesn't he? He slept until nearly nine o'clock and ate an enormous breakfast. We had ours in the sitting-room by the fire. Your father counts every moment lost that he doesn't spend in that sitting-room. In fact, he's so delighted with the whole house that he talks now of making this our headquarters for the summer . . ."

"Oh, Mom, couldn't we?" Mary Lee was all eagerness.

Her mother looked at her, surprised.

"But darling, I was afraid you'd be disappointed! You were so devoted to London."

"London," echoed Mary Lee. "Oh, yes, London was nice . . . But not nearly so nice as Somerhaze." A bright idea occurred to her. "You know, Mother," she pointed out, "this would be a wonderful place to—to concentrate on my school work. It's such a big house, I could get off by myself to study. It's ideal, sort of."

"So-o-o," drawled Mrs. Wade. "you're anxious to begin studying all of a sudden. In that case, I think I'll go in to Bridgwater with your father when he goes back to London this afternoon and buy pencils and pads and things so you can get right to work to-morrow. You can unpack your books while Pat has his rest. I'd rather you'd stay within call, if you don't mind, Mary Lee." She paused, then added, "It would be fun if I had tea with Dad in Bridgwater."

Mary Lee had meant to go out to the paddock again to watch Gillian and her brother "school" the ponies. Mom would be gone all afternoon if she had tea with Dad. Then she remembered the ten days in London—how little time her parents had had together. Her mother certainly deserved a treat now.

Pat's rest turned into a long nap. After tea it rained and was so chilly that Mary Lee kept him amused by the sitting-room fire for the remainder of the afternoon.

And so she didn't meet Jeffrey Randall until the following day.

She ran out of doors early—very early, before her seven-thirty breakfast. And she was alone because Gillian was preparing Mrs. Wade's tea-tray.

Jeffrey was feeding a pair of lambs. On his knees, his blond head bent over the pleasant task, he fended one little creature off while the other tugged at the big rubber-tipped nursing bottle he held under his arm.

Mary Lee was sure it was Jeffrey; he was so like his sister. Because she wore rubber-soled shoes he didn't hear her approach and she stood still for a moment watching the scene. Never, she thought, had she looked at anything so endearing as those lambs! They had black faces and black legs and their fleece was thick as thick!

"Oh," begged Mary Lee softly, "couldn't I? Oh, do let me feed them. I'll be so careful."

The boy, still on his knees, looked up and smiled. His eyes were bluer than his sister's, his hair an even paler yellow. He was not startled by Mary Lee's silent approach or her sudden impulsive plea.

"Why not?" he said. "Here's the bottle, but feed the other little beggar now. This one's had his share. And go slow or he may get the hiccups."

Mary Lee plumped down on her knees beside him and took the bottle he handed her. The lambs were not at all timid and the second one was soon sucking greedily.

The boy and girl were silent, intent on what they were doing. When the bottle was drained to the last drop, they stood up.

Mary Lee's well-developed social sense suddenly returned.

"I'm Mary Lee Wade," she said, "and I knew you must be Jeffrey Randall because you're a lot like Gillian. She told me about you yesterday. We're staying at the farm, you know."

"Yes, of course I know." Jeff grinned. He seemed a little amused by Mary Lee's formal manner. "Gill told me you were around yesterday. I helped her with the ponies for an hour or so after lunch. She said you and your brother wanted to ride."

"Oh, I do," Mary Lee told him. "But I don't know if Pat ought to. He's been ill for a long time."

"Do him a lot of good, I should think," Jeff said. "And Gill knows what she's about with riding—she'll look after him all right."

Mary Lee's attention returned to the lambs. "When do you feed them again?" she asked. "Would you—couldn't I help?"

Jeff's reply was, "Why not? Come along at about four o'clock. I'll wait for you. The old ewe had triplets this time and these two weren't very strong so Nannie's been hand-raising them. Only I mostly do it for her. They're coming along like anything now, aren't they?"

Boy and girl laughed together as they watched the lambs cavorting on the grass, following each other in what appeared to be a jumping contest.

"Little sillies," murmured Mary Lee.

"You're going to be late for breakfast," Jeff reminded her. "If Gran wasn't expecting you, I'd say come in and have it with Nan and me . . . What's more," he added, glancing skyward at grey clouds rolling down off the Quantocks, "you'd better run for it, if you don't want a soaking."

Mary Lee, without another word, turned and ran. The rain caught her before she reached the house, but it was only a silver shower after all.

And somewhere, out across the pastures, the cuckoo called and called again.

6. *The First Ride*

MARY LEE and Gillian had their first ride together that afternoon, Mrs. Wade having exacted a promise from each that they'd go carefully.

"You'd better put on something warm," Gillian warned at lunch-time. "I'll take you up Butterfly Combe and there'll be a cold wind when we get to the top."

So Mary Lee joined her a few minutes later wearing frontier pants, a bright red sweater and a tweed jacket.

"Ken's saddling the ponies for us," Gillian said. "I usually do it myself but we ought to get an early start if we're to be back before tea. Besides,

I told Pat I'd give him a turn round the paddock after we come in."

"Who's Ken?" asked Mary Lee.

"Ken . . . Oh, his name is Hawkins—Ken Hawkins—and he lives here, in the old shepherd's hut up by the beech wood. He was one of the boys who got sent to the country from London during the war—and when the others went back, there was no one to claim him. Either his people had been killed in a blitz or they just didn't want him any more."

"How awful!" exclaimed Mary Lee. She couldn't even remember the war, but it had taken Ken's home and family. And Gillian's father, too. For a moment it seemed very recent, very dreadful.

"Yes," Gillian agreed. "I suppose so, but Ken was lucky, in a way. Mummy and Gran were so sorry for him that they kept him on. And, even though he was just a kid, he was a lot of help when they were short-handed. He's got a magic way with animals. Children, too. Jeff and I used to follow him everywhere—like the dogs. Nannie disapproved like anything, of course." Gillian ended with a laugh.

"Why 'of course'?"

"Oh, she said it wasn't 'suitable.' I still do heaps of things that Nannie doesn't like. Jeff's her pet because he's like our father—or so everyone says."

By this time they had reached the paddock gate where a tall, lean young man stood waiting with the two ponies and a black and white bobtailed sheep dog. He gave Mary Lee a straight, unsmiling glance and the dog avoided her offered pat. Not a very friendly pair, she thought.

"Miss Mary Lee is all the way from America, Ken," Gillian told him, "and she hasn't ridden a lot so she'll take Bramble to-day."

"That's right," he agreed, and flicked her up on the pony's back as if she'd been a five-year-old. "I put a martingale on him, just in case. If the young lady ain't used to ponies, she'll be the better for it. They're pisky little beasts." He kept a hand on Bramble's rein as he went through the gate sideways.

"What did he mean by 'pisky'?" Mary Lee asked as they rode along the cart-track a moment later. "And these ponies aren't so little either. Horses, I'd call them."

"They're under fourteen-two," Gillian assured her. "Our Quantock ponies are a bit larger than Exmoors. We'll probably see some when we get up above the combe . . . Don't let Ken's word 'pisky' worry you; it only means sort of quick."

Mary Lee's first nervousness was forgotten in her excitement at the possibility of seeing wild ponies.

"And will there be colts with them, do you think?" she asked Gillian.

"Sure to be. Spring foals," was the answer.

They pulled up where the village lane met the main road.

Here stood the old inn called the Heart-in-Hand. Very solid it looked, with its small deep-set windows and heavy buttresses.

"That's a lovely place to have tea," Gillian volunteered. "Or ginger beer, on a hot day. Jeff and I come here for a treat sometimes. They do cream teas—with strawberries. Oh, de-e-licious they are! The landlord, Mr. Dinwiddy, is a great friend of ours and always piles on the cream."

One of the big green buses rumbled by on the main road and Gillian reached over and took Bramble's rein.

"You don't mind?" she asked, smiling. "The ponies aren't afraid of traffic but we have to follow the road a little way here—and I promised your mother to take care of you, remember."

They turned off, almost at once, up a cattle-track that led to a field. Mary Lee watched admiringly while Gillian brought Skittles up to a wooden gate, unlatched it and got them both through without dismounting. She carefully latched the gate again behind them.

"Gosh! that's smart!" was Mary Lee's comment.

Gillian apparently took this as a compliment to her pony.

"Oh, Bramble will do it, too," she said. "Only you have to be quick. If you miss the latch it's hard to bring them up the second time. It's awfully important to latch gates; farmers hate you if you don't. You'll remember that if you ride alone, won't you, Mary Lee?"

"Yes. Oh, yes, I'll be very careful," promised Mary Lee, mentally picturing an irate farmer pursuing her with a pitchfork as she and Bramble fled before him. She hoped Bramble was a good *fast* pony.

Gillian led the way at a footpace across the big, open field to another gate.

"I want you and Bramble to get used to each other," she said. "We can canter over this bit coming home. The ponies won't be so fresh then and, if he should try to get away with you, that first gate will stop him. I'll let you have a go at opening it," she added generously.

Mary Lee hoped—oh, how she hoped!—that Bramble would make no attempt to "get away" with her. If he did, would the gate be any hindrance to his mad flight?

"These ponies," she said quaveringly, "they can jump, can't they, Gillian? I mean, over gates and things?"

"Oh, they aren't too bad," Gillian answered indifferently. "I've never put them at anything very high; just a couple of poles in the paddock. I'd better get down to it pretty soon, though—those girls might want to enter them in some of the summer shows. . . . Now this is where the combe begins, Mary Lee. We'll have to go single file here."

She went ahead. They were on a grassy path, from either side of which the rounded hills, covered with rough vegetation, rose sharply.

"It's a wonderful sight in the autumn," Gillian called back over her shoulder, "when the gorse and heather is in bloom. Of course you only see bracken now."

"Is that green stuff bracken?" shouted Mary Lee. "I'd call it fern."

The path led on and on, always mounting. They splashed through a little clear stream that crossed it again and again. They rode past small grassy glades where groups of trees flaunted young green leaves.

"Perfect for picnics," Gillian said. And, a moment later, "I think we'll strike up for the top here. There's a good track, not too steep. Give that pony all the rein he wants now. It's a bit rough but don't worry, he's as sure-footed as a goat."

Mary Lee did as she was told, wishing at times that Bramble's mane offered a handhold. It had, alas, been hogged clean off!

But she gave a gasp of delight as they came out on top.

The great rugged hills rolled off in every direction, now blue, now green, sometimes deep purple where cloud shadows lay over them, obscuring all detail. Some of the slopes were heavily wooded and one saw the deep, mysterious combes leading down into the valley. Far away, in full sunshine, were fields spread out like a map—green fields and red-brown ones with trees and hedges separating one from another. And, in the uttermost distance, a silvery glint of water.

"Is it the sea, Gillian?" Mary Lee spoke in a hushed voice. There was something about this glorious upland with the cold, fresh wind blowing across it that made her feel very small. As if she and Gillian and the two ponies might be the only living creatures in an empty world.

"Yes," Gillian answered her. "Most people call it the Bristol Channel but there's a better name for it, one I love—'The Severn Sea.' The Welsh coast shows up on a really clear day, and sometimes at night the lights at Cardiff, right away on the other side. We'd better move along now. The ponies oughtn't to stand long in this wind. They're hot from the climb."

"But, Gillian," Mary Lee said, a little awkwardly, because she couldn't put what she felt into words, "I—I haven't thanked you for bringing me up here. It's—it's pretty gorgeous, isn't it?"

"I thought you might like it," was Gillian's quiet answer. "I never ride 'up over' without being grateful to God for letting me be born in the Quantock country."

Mary Lee remembered another country; a land of larger fields, of broader streams and blue, towering mountains.

"That," she said loyally, "is the way I feel about Virginia."

"Right, too," agreed Gillian, gathering up her reins.

Both ponies had raised their heads, pricked their ears as they moved forward, Skittles in the lead, for they must continue single file up here.

Gillian twisted round in the saddle.

"Look, Mary Lee—off to the left there! Hill ponies!"

"O—o-h!" breathed Mary Lee softly. "Can we get closer to them? Really close, do you think?"

"Yes. They're quite used to people. But they won't let you touch them. I've tried—often."

Four mares were feeding on the rough patches of grass among the bracken, their foals beside them. They raised their heads and stared as the girls approached, then moved slowly away. The foals showed more interest, cocking their little round ears, but kept close to their mothers' sides.

"We won't stop," Gillian said. "They'll only trot off, if we do. That little light-coloured foal is rather a poppet, isn't he?"

They rode on in silence for a short way. When the track widened and the ponies were side by side once more, Gillian spoke. "You know, Mary Lee," she said gravely, "I've got a sort of plan—for when I grow up, I mean. I—I—want to teach riding . . . Oh, I know it sounds silly now because I'm only twelve, but I love horses and I'm better at riding than anything else. I don't want to seem cocky, but I believe I've got a talent for it. Jeff thinks so too," she ended, a little defiantly.

Mary Lee looked at her. Gillian sat her pony so easily, so confidently in her faded old jodhpurs and shabby jacket. There was a wistful expression in the grey-blue eyes, as if she were seeking approval of her scheme. Well, she should have it.

"It's a *grand* idea," Mary Lee said. "You've got a perfect set-up for it right there at Somerhaze—with the old stable and the paddock and all. What does your mother think?"

"Oh, I haven't mentioned it to Mummy, only Jeff. But I'll tell you who would have backed me up—my granddad. He taught me to ride when I wasn't much more than a baby, and he was always awfully bucked when I did well at the gymkhanas and horse shows. He died only a year and a half ago. I still miss him a lot. . . ."

"You couldn't begin until you get through school, of course." Mary Lee was trying to be both practical and sympathetic.

"Oh, no. I'll have to go on through grammar school—which is a great bore."

"Where is it? The school, I mean."

"At Bridgwater. I'm a 'day girl.' I've only been there since I took my eleven plus exams last year."

Mary Lee was glad to hear that Gillian was a

day girl; she'd be at home at evenings and week-ends then.

"And Jeff? He goes away to school, doesn't he?" she asked.

"Yes, he's at his public school now. But he's got a scholarship. He swotted like anything his last term at prep. school because his masters thought he might get one and he did. We were all awfully bucked about it; full tuition would have been ghastly expensive."

"But I thought public schools were free," Mary Lee broke in, astonished. "Ours are."

"Oh, no," Gillian looked astonished in her turn. "State schools are the free schools in England. Mine is a State school."

"How odd!"

"How queer!" said the two girls in one breath.

Gillian laughed. "Anyway," she went on, "that's how we got the new bathroom. The minute Mummy knew Jeff's scholarship was safe she had it put in. We fought over it for a month—Jeff and I—because he claimed he'd earned it and I hadn't any right to use it. It was a riot.

"Look, this is where we go down into the combe again. The track is steep, so tighten your knees and don't slide off over Bramble's head."

The path was steep. Mary Lee not only tightened her knees but held her breath much of the way and was relieved when the grassy path was reached once more.

The canter across the field was accomplished without incident. "You're not too bad, you know, Mary Lee," Gillian said as they pulled up at the lower gate. "You and Bramble are going to suit each other very well."

Mary Lee, breathless from the excitement of her canter, gasped out a "Thanks."

"And you'll tell me if I do anything awfully wrong, won't you, Gillian? Shall I try opening the gate now?"

She fumbled the latch the first time but Bramble obligingly permitted a second attempt. Mary Lee was almost pulled out of the saddle as she dragged the gate back but she righted herself, giggling, and got through.

"Jolly good for a first try!" Gillian told her. "I *said* you'd get on all right with that pony, didn't I?"

They were soon back at the farm, to find Pat seated on the paddock fence.

"I thought you were never coming!" he greeted them. "I've been waiting for hours!"

Mary Lee slid off Bramble's back and Pat scrambled up from the stile.

"You've missed tea but they're keeping some hot for you," he called, as the two ponies moved off, Gillian's hand on Bramble's rein.

"Tea! What time is it then?"

"Nearly five o'clock."

"My lambs!" gasped Mary Lee, and raced away in the direction of Nannie's cottage.

7. *The Mangel House*

DAY FOLLOWED pleasant day at Somerhaze Farm.

Mary Lee and Pat settled to a routine of morning work and afternoon play.

Since Gillian was always busy in the mornings and studying must be faced, Mary Lee found the arrangement a pleasanter one than she had expected. Her mother had a knack of making lessons interesting.

Afternoon rides continued; up other combes and other hills, or across pasture and meadow land. And Gillian nearly always gave Pat a half-hour's coaching in the paddock when they came home.

"It wouldn't surprise me," she told Mary Lee, "if that boy made a rider. He's got a lot of confidence already, and he pays attention to what he's doing. He goes better at the trot than you do, Mary Lee, and he'll have nice light hands, I think. Most beginners hold on by the reins, you know."

"Do I?" asked Mary Lee, surprised and a little hurt. "You show Pat more than you do me, Gillian."

"Perhaps I do," Gillian agreed thoughtfully. "I daresay you'd be the better for an afternoon in the paddock. I can stand off and watch you then; when we're out on the hills there's so much to see and talk about that I don't notice how you're riding. Let's do it to-morrow, shall we?"

They did. And Mary Lee learned a lot. She felt she'd have learned even more if Pat hadn't stood around adding his criticism to Gillian's. After all, a small brother is a small brother and one can stand only so much. Her impatience began to affect the pony and he got his head down, pulling hard.

"Ease up on your rein, Mary Lee!" Gillian shouted. "He's going to buck you off, if you don't."

At that moment Ken appeared, his approach as silent and unexpected as usual.

"I'm goin' up to my hut for a cuppa tea," he announced. "You can come along with me if you want to, Pat."

Pat attached himself to Ken at once and Gillian threw him a grateful smile.

"And that just shows how useful Ken can be," she said. "Now, get down off that pony before you try his temper too far. I'll put you up on Posy, I think. She's got the sweetest manners and a very light mouth. You'll love her."

Posy was a good big mare and Mary Lee felt herself a long way off the ground, but before they had circled the paddock twice, she was charmed with her.

"You see," Gillian explained, at the end of the lesson, "Jeff and I are the only ones who ride Posy. She's young—rising five—but she knows just what we expect of her. Ponies are usually headstrong and these two have had all sorts of riders. Bramble will have forgotten his sulks by to-morrow. And so will you."

Mary Lee laughed as she patted the mare's dappled neck.

"My kid brother's a pest sometimes," she said. "He got me all riled up just now. But you know, Gillian, I believe you're right about teaching riding. You've got a talent for it."

Gillian blushed with pleasure but all she said was, "Oh, it's only a matter of patience, really."

Mrs. Wade, in response to her daughter's urging, attended a feeding of the lambs. She was amused and pleased with the little creatures, but she soon drifted into a conversation with Jeff on the subject of farming.

Mary Lee, half-listening, was reminded of home and her mother's way with young students from

Dad's classes at the University. So now her daughter was not surprised to hear Jeff telling about the dairy herd, how his grandfather had encouraged him to farm the land, of his hopes and plans for the future.

"Of course, Buffin and Ken do the actual work now," he said. "But I usually fetch the cows to and from pasture when I'm home. That way I've got to know every one and, this summer, when the long holiday begins, I'm going to help with the milking. You haven't seen the milking yet, have you, Mrs. Wade? It's—well, I think it's rather interesting."

Mrs. Wade promptly arranged to attend evening milking next day.

Mary Lee went out to the old cow barn with her. She was not quite happy when the big red and white beasts came ambling past, especially as two or three stopped to stare at her, breathing heavily; but Jeff told her they were only curious because she and her mother were strangers.

"Cows have heaps of curiosity," he said. "They've got to find out about everything or anybody that's different."

All the same Mary Lee was glad when each had taken her place in a familiar stall, a metal stanchion had been clamped on her neck and the feed before her occupied her full attention.

The milking machines were brought in, and work began.

Mary Lee soon tired of the milking and wandered

off. She had a look at Pat's pigs (she always thought of them as Pat's pigs) and hung over the pen where the three young calves lived. Two were Ayrshires, one a Jersey—Venus's youngest child, she thought.

Her mother and Jeffrey overtook her in the farmyard as she was peering into a little circular building with a pointed roof of thatch. Inside were some odds and ends of farm machinery, a bicycle, baskets, a couple of twig brooms.

"What is this place?" she asked. "I've wondered ever since I've been here but I keep forgetting to ask Gillian. I mean, what was it built for?"

"It's the old mangel house."

"And I can only hope you're wiser than you were before, Mary Lee." Her mother laughed. "I confess, I'm not."

"Don't you have mangels in the States?" Jeff seemed surprised. "Mangold-wurzels is the proper name—they're big, tough root vegetables. Very good for sheep, and they used to feed them to cattle too—chipped up. This place was for chipping them. A horse, or an ox, was hitched to a sort of windlass and led round and round while a machine cut the mangels with a sharp blade. Most old farms have mangel houses but they aren't used that way any more. Gill and I played in this one when we were kids. We brought tea out here, especially when our Cary cousins came over. We'd build a little fire to keep it hot, but of course the smoke always choked us and we'd have to stamp it out. And the Carys made us wild because they'd talk about their gazebo at the Court. Well, it is a jolly thing to look at —same period as the house—and it has a real fireplace, and furniture, but it's too elegant by half. Gill and I liked the mangel house best."

"It would make a *darling* playhouse," Mary Lee said enthusiastically, "with a few chairs and a table and a rug, maybe. I mean," she added, suddenly remembering her thirteen years, "if we weren't too old for that sort of thing"

Perhaps it was just as well that she missed the amused glance that passed between her mother and Jeffrey.

"Are we too old, I wonder?" he asked. "I'm moving up to the house this evening, you know, and I was thinking we might clear out the old mangel house to-morrow. If we stuck in a few bits and pieces, it would make a good bolt hole, come the summer holidays. A spot to escape to in case there are a lot of people about, I mean."

It then occurred to him that Mrs. Wade, whose good opinion he very much valued, would naturally assume that she was included among "a lot of people," and he blushed.

"I mean," he stammered, "what I really meant was—well, Mum told me that Mr. Wade is writing a book—and we, especially Pat, could get ourselves out of the way if we made the old mangel house a sort of headquarters."

Mary Lee could hardly wait for him to finish.

"Oh, do let's!" she exclaimed excitedly. It was an expression of approval she'd caught from Gillian.

Her mother put Jeff at ease by ignoring his desperate explanation and returning to the subject of the gazebo.

"I've never seen one," she said, "and I'm sure my husband would be interested. His book is connected with architecture. Is Cary Court near here?"

"Oh, yes. At Stogary. That's the next village—about a mile—but there's a footpath across the fields which makes it less than that. The Court's a school for little girls now. Gill went there until last year. It's a great barn of a place—Regency, I think. Anyway, the Carys couldn't carry on. So they live in the gate-house now, with enough land for a garden and a bit of lawn. They'd be glad to show you the gazebo; the house, too, for that matter, but I wouldn't go there in term time, it's positively seething with kids. School begins again pretty soon."

"Oh," exclaimed Mary Lee, "you'll be going back, won't you? And Gill, too, until nearly August. How horrid!"

"Oh, I don't know," Jeff said, kicking a small stone as he spoke. "School's not bad. I miss the farm, of course, but then I sort of forget about it—there's so much to do. Games and all that. I might get down here for Whitsun week-end—and there's the half-term break."

"I think Mary Lee meant it would be horrid for her," Mrs. Wade told him. "With you and Gillian both away."

"Oh, well, Gill will be here evenings. It'll be light until all hours from now on and the girls can have their ride after tea. The ponies have got to be ridden anyway. And I'll tell you what," Jeff said, turning to Mary Lee, "you can take over the lambs! Nan will show you about the milk and you can feed 'em twice a day by yourself."

Mary Lee was so delighted with this suggestion that she forgot the possibility of her own loneliness.

8. *Common Heritage*

GRADUALLY, unobtrusively, Mary Lee and her mother took on a number of household tasks. When the Randalls protested, Mrs. Wade told them she had too much leisure on her hands. She and Mary Lee made their own beds and kept the bathroom neat, giggling together over the "airing cupboard" where the sheets and towels were kept, and at the row of hot-water bottles, each in its own little flannel jacket.

The Randalls assumed that a good hearty tea and early bedtime would continue for Pat and he made little protest, for he was healthily tired towards the end of each long, active day.

Supper was at seven-thirty. Afterwards the dishes were piled on the trolley, wheeled into the scullery and the three young people "washed up," according to Jeff and Gillian—"did the dishes," according to Mary Lee. Late as it was when they finished, the sun had not yet gone down and they often strolled as far as the duck pond in the mellow evening light before going to bed.

When Mr. Wade came from London for a long week-end he was pleased to find his family so happily settled, for he was still determined to make Somerhaze their headquarters.

"The West Country is full of historically interesting places," he told his wife. "When I come down to stay we'll take the children to see them. Meanwhile, why don't you join me for a few days in London now and then, Ginnie? Mary Lee is old enough to keep an eye on Pat." And his daughter quickly agreed that she was.

On Sunday the Wades went, with Jeff and Gillian, to morning service at the village church.

Pat elected to remain at the farm.

"Mother and I will go to Evensong if you don't mind supper being a bit late," Rose said. "But Jeff and Gill will see that you meet the Vicar after service. Our little church is very old, you know, and Mr. Aldrich is rather interesting on the subject of its history and architecture. Mr. Wade might enjoy a talk with him."

They approached the tiny stone church through a lich-gate and up a grassy walk between the yew hedge and a wall, half-covered with white, pink and yellow blossoms.

Suddenly the bells burst forth; one series of joyous notes after another, filling the spring morning with such a melodious clamour that conversation was impossible.

Jeff, seeing Mary Lee's delight, led her into the small space directly under the tower to watch the shirt-sleeved ringers at work. Up and down, up and down went the ropes with their red sallies, each man varying his hold and timing as the changes rang out.

Mary Lee stood with parted lips and shining eyes, drinking in the glorious sound.

Jeff, after watching her for a moment, leaned over and half-shouted in her ear, "I'll take you up in the tower some day where you can see the bells swinging. Golly! You *can* hear 'em up there!" Then he added, "I'll have to nip along now, can't hold up the choir. We're only six in all."

The congregation rose as the choir, followed by the Vicar, filed in.

Gillian nudged Mary Lee and whispered, "That's Mr. Dinwiddy, the one with the whiskers. He's got a splendid bass voice. The two little boys are the naughtiest ones in the village, the Muggridge twins. Look like cherubs now, don't they? The young man next to Jeff is Mr. Chilcott's grandson—'Our Stan'—he rides a horrible motor-bike all the time. And the old man is

Mr. Clatworthy who can't sing for toffee—just quavers—but he's always been in the choir and always will be, I should think."

Mary Lee was longing to hear more about these village characters, but the Vicar was beginning with "Dearly beloved Brethren, the Scripture moveth us in sundry places . . ." and she thought she'd better concentrate. She kept her eyes on her Prayer Book for, though she'd been brought up an Episcopalian and her mother had said her church was directly descended from the Church of England, there was just enough difference in the service to make her wary. The prayer for "Our Gracious Sovereign Lady, Queen Elizabeth," she was prepared for and heartily approved, thinking it romantic, but the older wording of many familiar passages was something to trip over. The Vicar's intoning surprised her because she'd never encountered it before, but she decided it was pleasing when one got used to it.

Gillian, beside her, was word-perfect, of course, her serene blue gaze often wandering as she made the responses in her pretty clipped voice.

During the sermon Mary Lee relaxed, and in spite of herself, her attention strayed. There was so much to look at. The high wooden pulpit, approached by a flight of steps, the old carved pew ends, each a different design: leaves, flowers, grapes, and the most grotesque birds and beasts on occasional ones. Then the angels. There were angels everywhere! Small wooden ones with outspread wings terminated the graceful beams supporting the roof. They appeared in the glass of the stone-traceried windows and small kneeling angels topped the posts of the little choir stalls beyond the delicate chancel screen. Fat marble cherubs decorated an elaborate memorial tablet on the opposite wall.

Mary Lee gave a little start as she slowly made out the wording below the cherubs—"Near this place lyeth the bodye of Chloe Randall—beloved wife of Hugh Neville Randall, Gent." The dates following were unreadable, blurred by time, but surely this must be the Chloe whose portrait hung in the dining-room at Somerhaze.

Just above the pew where Mary Lee sat was a new and simple brass plaque. The words on it were all too easy to read: "In loving memory of Mark Neville Randall, Flight-Lieut., R.A.F.—Born, 1919—Killed in Action, 1944." Gillian's and Jeff's father. No wonder the Randalls were "fond" of this church, as Rose had said: it seemed to knit the family together over so many years.

Would the sermon never be over?

It was at last, and Mary Lee was pleased to recognise the hymn to follow, a favourite of hers; "The Spacious Firmament on High."

She was singing with a will when a small embroidered velvet bag, looking for all the world like a lady's vanity case, was thrust under her nose.

"Offertory!" whispered Gillian in her ear and

Mary Lee hastily dropped in the shilling she'd been holding, forgotten, in her hand for some time. But surely the offertory came before the sermon at home—and one put it on a silver collection plate? She was glad to hide her embarrassment by kneeling for the Benediction.

The Vicar was standing in the doorway as they went out, smiling and shaking hands with his parishioners. Gillian introduced the Wade family and he and Mr. Wade turned back into the church almost at once.

"They'll be talking about hammer beam roofs and rood screens for the next half-hour," Mrs. Wade said. "I think I'll stroll on and see if I can help about dinner."

Jeff who had joined them decided to go with her.

Mary Lee promptly led Gillian to the Chloe memorial.

"Yes, that's our Chloe all right," Gillian said in answer to her excited questions. "I think 'this place' means she was buried under the floor—they often did that in those days See—this is another ancestor," and she indicated a stone slab near the chancel step. "But it's been walked over so much you can hardly make out the letters—just a J and a Y—another Jeffrey probably. All the Randalls seem to have been Jeffrey or Mark or Hugh. That's my father's brass plaque over our pew; he was Mark you know."

"Yes. I noticed it right away," Mary Lee said

shyly, "but I wasn't going to say anything about it to you."

"Why ever not?" asked Gillian, looking surprised.

"I thought it might make you feel sad."

"Oh, no. We're awfully proud of him—Jeff and I. But we can't miss him. You can't miss what you've never known, can you? Mummy must do, of course—and Gran. I know how they feel because I was awfully unhappy when Granddad died. But they're lucky to have Jeff."

"They're lucky to have you, too," Mary Lee declared.

"Yes. But I know I'm not as important as Jeff is. Oh, they love me as much as they do him but I'm not so important—that's all."

"You aren't?" asked Mary Lee. "Why not?"

"Oh, well, I'm a girl. I might get married some day and stop being a Randall. Jeff will carry on at Somerhaze and look after Mummy always. Gran says he has a great sense of responsibility. He's awfully decent to me, too, backing me up with my plan for a riding school and all that."

"What I think is, half the farm ought to be yours."

"Oh, no," Gillian protested. "that wouldn't be right." A smile flickered over her face. "My father left me a present, though—and a message just as he went out of the gate on his last leave at home, Mummy said."

"What were they?" Mary Lee asked. "Or would you rather not say?"

"I don't mind *you* knowing." And Mary Lee was flattered by the accent on the "you." "The message was, 'Tell our daughter to be happy.' He seemed to know I was going to be a girl, you see. And the present was a button off his tunic. It had got loose, and Mummy had sewed a new one on for him the night before. He'd dropped the old one in his pocket and he left it with her—for me. I'll show it to you when we get home."

"I'd like to see it," Mary Lee said gently. "And are you happy—always?"

"I try to be. I thought about it when I was confirmed—when I promised to honour my father and mother, you know."

Mary Lee who had, up till now, thought Gillian strangely indifferent to her father's death, suddenly changed her mind.

And Gillian didn't forget to show her the button. She came into Mary Lee's room with it in her hand just beforc tea, a plain brass button with an albatross, surmounted by the royal crown.

"I wear it sometimes," Gillian told her. "On a ribbon round my neck, when I think I might be afraid of something. School exams—or at a really good horse show when the jumps might be a bit sticky. It helps. Everyone in the R.A.F. must have been awfully brave."

Mary Lee understood. The tiny present, given so lightly by a young father, was of tremendous value to the daughter he had never seen. From that moment she loved Gillian Randall.

The following week Gillian went back to school. Jeff departed a few days later, his mother driving him to the Bridgwater station in the Biscuit Tin.

"Glad you'll be here to play around with old Gilly," he told Mary Lee just before he left. "She doesn't have too much fun."

Mary Lee lost some of the indignation she had felt because Jeff owned a farm and Gillian a brass button. After all, it was not his fault—just the way things had happened. And he was very fond of his sister.

Throughout the countryside May brought its wealth of blossom. Hawthorn, pink and white, in the hedges, campion and stitchwort, (though Mary Lee preferred the country name of "milk-maids,") lined the lanes and the meadows were as golden as ever with the buttercups treading on the heels of the dandelions.

"'The Field of the Cloth of Gold,'" Gillian said, one perfect Saturday afternoon when she and Mary Lee rode across one of these flowery pastures under a pale-blue, rain-washed sky. "I always think of that when I see the buttercups, though I know old Henry VIII showing off before the King of France was something quite different."

"I wish I knew my English history the way you do," Mary Lee said wistfully. "I've got as far as

Richard III and the Wars of the Roses though, and it's awfully interesting because I saw the film on the ship coming over. You're always being reminded of history in this country. It's all around you, sort of."

She waved a hand vaguely.

"What I don't know about American history would fill a book," Gillian announced. "Absolutely nothing, except that the colonies got annoyed with us and we fought a war about it. And Davy Crockett, of course. You can't dodge hearing about him now, can you?"

"Goodness!" exclaimed Mary Lee. "Don't you know about our Civil War? The one that freed the slaves? Or about the pioneers going west all the time to settle new country? That part is awfully exciting. But it was such a little while ago compared to your history. Why, your church was standing where it is now when Columbus discovered America! And Dad says your house was probably being built while the Pilgrims were scrambling up Plymouth Rock! Just think!"

They both thought for a moment in silence.

"When did your people go to America?" Gillian asked suddenly. "I mean your father's and mother's people—and did they come from the British Isles?"

"Ye-es, I think so," Mary Lee said slowly, trying to remember what her parents had told her. "Oh, yes, the Wades came to Virginia from England, I'm sure, and Mother's family was Scottish."

"Right! Now just listen a minute, Mary Lee, because it's important, English history is *your* history just as much as it's ours, up to about two hundred years ago—or maybe less. And literature, too, Chaucer and Shakespeare and—and Sir Philip Sidney, I dare say. Your people helped to build the castles and abbeys and everything, just as ours did. So it all belongs to you, in the same way, you see."

They had pulled their ponies to a halt and now sat staring at each other while Mary Lee puzzled over what Gillian had just said.

"Gosh, Gill!" she exclaimed at last. "It's true! Funny, I hadn't thought of it like that before."

"Nor had I," Gillian admitted. "But our English lit. mistress said something only a few days ago about America and us having what she called a 'common heritage'—all of you who came from here and speak our language anyway."

"Swell, isn't it?" said Mary Lee, beaming.

"Smashing, I'd call it."

Their mood changed. Action was what was wanted.

"Race you to the far end of this field, Mary Lee," Gillian challenged.

Mary Lee clapped her heels into Bramble's sides and was off before the words were finished.

But she was far from Gillian's equal as a rider, and Skittles was the faster of the two ponies. They thundered alongside, then swept past before half the distance was covered, Gillian laughing back over her shoulder.

"Your riding has improved no end, though," she said as Mary Lee brought Bramble to a reluctant stop. "Some day soon we'll exchange ponies and race them again. They need a bit of waking up before the summer shows begin. Would you like to go home by the Bluebell Wood?"

Oh, yes, Mary Lee wanted to go by the Bluebell Wood. She thought it might be pretty. But she had not expected the delicate, shimmering lake of pure blue that met her eyes; a pool of blue lapping the smooth grey boles of the beech trees, still wearing the young green leaves of spring.

The two girls gazed their fill without speaking.

"It's just as if the sky had fallen through," said Mary Lee at last. "Could I pick some, Gill? I'd like to take them home to Mother."

"I wouldn't; they wilt," Gillian told her, "like any wild thing that you take indoors. Bring your mother up here to-morrow instead—it isn't far—and bluebells ought to be seen all together, like this, you know."

Gillian was right, of course. But the Bluebell Wood was so unbelievably lovely that Mary Lee half-feared it would have vanished by next day.

They rode quietly over the final pasture because Gillian said the ponies wanted cooling off after their gallop.

It was here that they heard the skylark. High

overhead it was, and circling higher but never ceasing its wild, ecstatic song. Mary Lee watched until she could no longer see the tiny body and still she heard it singing.

"Gill," she whispered, "is that really a bird—the 'Blithe Spirit' one?"

"That's him. 'Hark! Hark! the lark at Heaven's gate sings,' and so on. You needn't get too excited about him, though, you'll probably hear him every day right through June." She smiled understandingly and added, "The bluebells will be with us for at least a fortnight, too."

But Mary Lee was thinking, *my* skylark, *my* Bluebell Wood! Because her people, long and long ago, had listened to larks and seen the bluebells, they were as surely hers as the mocking birds and crape myrtle of her native Virginia. And it was Gillian—generous Gillian—who had opened her eyes to their common heritage.

They rode on, through the evening light, towards a grey mist that was wood smoke rising from the tall chimneys of Somerhaze Farm.

9. Tea with Nannie

IT WAS at Nannie Chilcott's cottage that Mary Lee heard again of the Somerhaze ghost.

Pat had formed the habit of dropping in for tea with Nannie.

"I like her, and she has such scrumptious teas," he explained.

And Mrs. Randall urged his mother to let him go.

"Nannie's never really happy without a child around," she said. "She can't, or won't, realise that Jeff and Gillian are growing up. Pat will keep her from feeling neglected."

Mary Lee had been in Nannie's cosy little kitchen a time or two to watch her prepare the milk for the lambs. But the lambs were no longer bottle-fed and had been moved to the orchard to crop the long grass there. They still gambolled towards her under a drifting shower of white petals when she visited them, but soon they were to join the other sheep in the big upper pasture. Sad, Mary Lee thought, but she was comforted by their look of sturdiness, knowing she had helped to make them so.

When Pat told his sister that Nannie would like her to come to tea with him next day, one would have thought it a royal command.

"You're not to wear pants," he said firmly. "Nannie likes ladies to be ladies. She can't bear girls in pants."

"But I'm going to ride with Gill right afterward," Mary Lee protested. "Gill wears jodhpurs all the time, practically. And she looks better in them than she does in skirts."

"Nannie doesn't think so. She says Mrs. Randall rode sidesaddle, in a proper habit—hunting and everything. She's got a picture of her at a Meet, with the Master and all the hounds. On a big black hunter she is, and she looks O.K. in a sidesaddle. There's one of Gill's father on his first pony, too; and one of him grown up, in his R.A.F. uniform. Nan keeps a little bunch of flowers in front of it."

So Mary Lee brushed her hair carefully and changed into her grey flannel suit. At the last moment she thrust a pair of white cotton gloves into one pocket and a clean handkerchief in the other.

She had expected tea in the kitchen; she knew Pat usually had it there, but now he led her through a picket gate and a gay little garden to the front door where their hostess met them.

Nannie's erectness, whether sitting or standing, gave her an air of great dignity, but her gentle blue eyes, soft white hair and softer Somerset country voice were always reassuring.

This tea-party was obviously an occasion, for the two young guests were ushered into a tiny parlour, so stuffed with furniture and knick-knacks that Mary Lee could not help wondering how three people were to be fitted in. And she was surrounded by alarming hazards. One or more of the elaborately ruffled pillows overflowing the chairs might be catapulted on to the floor at any moment. If she made a gesture with either hand, a silver-framed photograph was bound to go. The starched white cloth, edged with yards of crocheted lace, which covered the little tea table simply invited disaster with jam.

She was worrried, too, about Pat, who edged his way between pieces of furniture to converse with a small, green bird in a cage.

"Nannie's budgie," Pat said it was. "Listen, Mary Lee, he can talk—he can say nursery rhymes. Come on, Georgy . . . Pretty bird, pretty bird . . ."

"Pretty bird, pretty bird," echoed Georgy. Then, "Georgy, porgy, puddin'y pie—kisses the girls an' makes 'em cry . . . Pretty bird . . . 'umpty, Dumpty, sat-on-a-wall . . . Pretty bird . . . Pretty Georgy. . . ."

Mary Lee laughed aloud; he sounded so proud of himself.

Nannie entered the room with a big brown teapot, popped a padded cosy over it and took her seat at the table.

Pat had spoken truly: the food was scrumptious. Split muffins, toasted and buttered, clotted cream and what Nannie said was a Victoria sandwich, two layers of spongecake with jam between and powdered sugar on top. Also ginger nuts, if one hadn't already eaten too many other things.

"I don't do much baking now," Nannie said. "It 'ardly seems worth it, like, not with Chidzey's van coming over from Stogary twice a week. I was never a one for cooking, unless some little special thing for one of my babies."

Mary Lee, having heard that Nannie had no children of her own, assumed that "my babies" referred to her nurslings, and began to ask questions about the pictures of children which cluttered the room.

Nothing could have pleased Nannie more. She showed Mary Lee dozens, it seemed; many of Jeff and Gillian, several of their father and a number of young Carys, for Nannie had spent some time at Cary Court between the generations at Somerhaze. To hear her talk one would have thought both places Paradise in what she called "the old days." Finally she shook her head, sighing.

"It makes my 'eart ache sometimes to see all Mrs. Randall and young Mrs. Mark 'as to do now." she said. "With only Polly Buffin in once a week for the roughs. Of course, things would 'ave been different if Mr. Mark 'adn't been taken the way 'e was—so young and all. I can't believe it's natural, Miss, for people to go flying around in the air but, I suppose, with a war on, it was called for. Mrs. Mark was very brave—she 'ad to be, with two babies to plan for. I did all I could for them in the 'ouse but they were short-'anded on the farm, too, with Ken no more than a lad and Buffin wardening nights to that extent 'e could 'ardly do a decent day's work. I used to think to myself that if ever their Mistress Chloe, that they set such store by, was going to bring a change of luck, then was the time . . ."

Nannie paused, noting Mary Lee's look of astonishment.

"'Aven't you never 'eard of the Zomer'aze ghost, dearie?" she asked.

"Ye-e-es." Mary Lee remembered their acquaintance on the train. "But—but—I didn't know it was Chloe. The lady in the picture, you mean?"

"That's right—Mistress Chloe Randall."

Pat who had been fiddling about with some pieces from an old ivory chess set, suddenly entered the conversation.

"Gosh, Nannie," he said, "she'd sure make a

wonderful ghost! I wish she'd show up while we're here. If I see her I'll . . ."

Then Nannie pounced.

"That's not a proper way to speak, Patrick," she said, severely. "'Gosh' isn't a word to use before ladies. And, as for Mistress Chloe, you'll not see 'er for she only appears to the Master of Zomer'aze, ever. Now, tell me you're sorry, nicely."

To his sister's surprise, Pat instantly murmured "Sorry, Nan," with a disarming grin.

But the spell was broken. Nannie began gathering up the tea things.

Mary Lee, doubly careful of her manners now (and remembering guiltily that she often said "Gosh" herself) not only thanked Nannie for her party, but said good-bye to Georgy, who preened himself and repeated "Pretty bird—pretty bird" several times.

When Mary Lee told her mother about the tea-party, Mrs. Wade made light of the ghost story. She was far more interested in a description of the cottage.

"But, Mom, do you think there really *is* a ghost?" Mary Lee asked.

"My dear, I wouldn't know. Anyway, according to Nannie, she can't appear to anyone but Jeffrey now. He owns this place, since his grandfather's death, which makes him Master of Somerhaze, I suppose. So you can put the whole thing out of your mind. Unless," Mrs. Wade added, with one of her mischievous smiles, "unless we ask Mrs. Randall to tell us more about Chloe sometime when your father's here; he's always interested in these old legends. It might make an amusing evening."

Such an evening was not offered until the Whitsun week-end, however.

Mr. Wade was with them and Jeff arrived on Friday to remain through the following Wednesday.

Gillian was in the gayest of moods. A holiday, her brother home for the better part of a week and, as if that wasn't enough, there was to be a small gymkhana at Stogary on Whit Monday afternoon. She was to ride Skittles in several of the classes. The fact that it rained a cold drizzle all morning did not dampen her ardour in the least.

"It's a great piece of luck," she told Mary Lee "that the girls who own our ponies don't want to ride them to-day. Know they're out of practice, I suppose, but they'll ask for them back this summer all right so I'll have to look about for something else. You can ride over with me on Bramble, if you like. You might be useful to walk Skittles between events and cool him off."

"Be your stableboy, you mean," teased Mary Lee.

"All right. Pat will be just as good."

"Mother wouldn't dream of turning Pat out on a day like this—it's only fit for ducks."

Jeff stood by, a grin on his face, listening to the argument.

"For goodness' sake, Mary Lee," he urged, "go—or she'll elect me for the part."

Gillian swung round on him.

"I'd forgotten you were here, Jeff," she said at once. "You'll do nicely. You can ride the mare over; I want to get her used to shows anyway."

It ended by all three riding across the dripping fields in mackintoshes, with collars turned up about their ears and their hands wet on the slippery reins.

Rose drove Pat around by the road in the Biscuit Tin.

"The top doesn't leak too badly, and it will make a shelter for the children at tea-time," she said, as she stowed a well-filled picnic basket in the back seat.

Gillian won the bending race and musical poles, and Mary Lee couldn't have been prouder if she'd done it herself. They walked their horses home in late watery sunlight with blue rosettes fluttering from Skittles's bridle.

Gillian was hilarious, laughing and chattering all the way.

"How I happened to win the bending event I can't imagine," she said, "with Mary Ann Lambert on her Badger. She and that pony go like blazes every time. I don't think anyone's ever got the potato race away from them—they're a great little team. The thing I'm actually thrilled about, though, is that Major Adcock has asked me to board a pony for his daughter. It's a four-year-old Connemara mare, and green. He thinks she's hardly up to handling it yet, so I'm to school it all summer."

"Good girl!" said Jeff. "That's the real reason you wanted to turn out for this show, wasn't it?"

Gillian nodded.

"After all, people can't know you're good with horses unless they see you ride," she said. "I—I only hoped something like that might happen—and it did."

"It means you've got what it takes," Mary Lee summed the matter up.

After supper the two families, with the exception of Pat, gathered round the fire in the sitting-room. And Mrs. Randall told them the story of Chloe's last visitation.

It was quite unplanned.

Mr. Wade had commented on Gillian's likeness to the portrait.

"Is that portrait by Peter Lely?" he asked. "I don't pretend to know much about pictures."

"Goodness, no!" Mrs. Randall replied. "We'd have been tempted to sell it if it was. We let two Morlands go to help with the children's school fees, but we've still got the Stubbs in the hall. I suppose we're lucky, really, to live in a good old house that isn't too large for us to manage, with no heirlooms of great value. They're a responsibility, yet one clings to them."

"What about Chloe's necklace?" Mrs. Wade asked. "It looks an exquisite thing."

"I've every reason to believe it was," Mrs. Randall told her. "There's a copy of it somewhere in the boxroom, along with a costume exactly like Chloe's. It was made for me when I came here as a bride to wear to a big country-house ball. It created a sensation; we were very gay then—times were easier. My new father-in-law gave me the necklace and I was so much impressed I wouldn't put it on until he told me it was only a Pinchbeck imitation of the original. *That* had gone during the Regency, for a gaming debt, probably. Gentlemen—and ladies, too—gambled so recklessly in those days, didn't they? I can't think why the copy was made, unless for some sort of record. But it's a pretty thing. Remind me and I'll get it out to show you while you're here."

"Maybe—maybe that's why Chloe comes back," suggested Jeff. "Maybe she's looking for her necklace."

"Nonsense, boy, she wouldn't bother with a trumpery thing such as we've got, and she's been seen since the Regency era, remember. Your great-grandfather saw her for one."

"Er—when was that?" asked Mr. Wade.

"Oh, sometime in the early nineties, I suppose—he was a young man at the time anyway. He told me about it soon after I married his son, which was towards the end of the first World War. We were great friends—Papa and I."

"*Do* go on, Mrs. Randall," begged Mary Lee. "She always brings luck, doesn't she—your Chloe? Nannie told me so."

"Yes. Poor Nan has been hoping she'd return and make a change in the family fortune for years. And she did bring Papa a bit of luck. He'd been considering a bet on a horse that was to race—at Doncaster, was it? Or the National? Anyway, he couldn't decide whether to back the favourite or another animal that he fancied, and the problem kept him awake. He slept in the big room, the one where you and Pat do your school-work now. It was the master bedroom then and the old bathroom next it was a dressing-room. Papa had blown out his candles, but there was a full moon so it was not really dark. He heard just a whisper of sound, like leaves rustling, though it was a still night. Then . . . Chloe drifted in through the dressing-room door. She looked just as she does in the portrait, and the little grey-hound followed her. She paused in a shaft of moonlight and smiled charmingly. He thought he called her by name but couldn't be sure of that. She said, and her voice was charming, too, 'I know what you want: back Harmony.' He thanked her, but she was gone the instant she finished speaking. He slept almost at once and, next morning, he placed his bet on Harmony without a qualm. He'd never given the horse a thought—it was a rank outsider, but it won *by three lengths*! And the most amazing thing was, it never won another race. So you see . . ."

There was a moment's silence.

"And what do we see?" asked Jeff. "That Great-grandpapa had one of those queer dreams nobody can explain. Oh, I don't say there mightn't be something in it . . ."

"He'd doubtless been mulling over a list of entries for this race and 'Harmony' was impressed on his subconscious mind," was Mr. Wade's explanation.

"Odd though, that the horse never won again, wasn't it?" said Rose. "I wonder what he did with his winnings."

"I can tell you that, too," Mrs. Randall said. "He bought those cherry brocade curtains in the dining-room. And *how* I have cherished them!"

Mary Lee, since her request for the story, had listened in silence but with eyes like saucers.

Rose, suddenly aware of her bemused state, suggested that a nice hot cup of tea all round would be welcome, and went out to make it.

When she returned with the tray she reported that it was raining again.

"So I'll have to make yet another trip to the attic and empty the old tin bath we keep under the spot where the roof leaks," she said ruefully. "If Mistress Chloe ever visits me and asks what I want, I'll plump for a load of nice new tiles."

But Jeff and Mr. Wade volunteered to empty the bath for her, which Rose said was almost as good.

10. *Garden Fête*

GILLIAN ASKED her brother to ride over to Major Adcock's place with her to lead the Connemara mare back to the farm.

"Jeff will help me cope if anything goes wrong," she confided to Mary Lee. "I don't know how this pony may behave on the road after the Irish bogs she's been used to."

And Mary Lee, looking round for something to do in their absence, encountered Mrs. Randall carrying a basket of roses in one hand and a cotton duster in the other.

"It's my month to do the flowers at the church," she said. "And I always take a duster for mopping up, if necessary. How would you like to come with me? These are our first rosebuds; for the altar and the ledge under our 'Roll of Honour.' And some rosemary for my husband's grave. 'Rosemary for Remembrance,' you know. He loved his Shakespeare."

Mary Lee recognised the old man from the choir, cutting the unkempt grass between the gravestones in the little churchyard even before Mrs. Randall greeted him with a cheery "Good morning, Mr. Clatworthy."

"This is a young friend of ours from America," she added. And to Mary Lee, "Wouldn't you rather stay outside in the sunshine with Mr. Clatworthy? Ours is a pretty churchyard and such a lovely view over the fields to the hills. My husband's grave is just along there . . . I'll be back presently."

How cheerful these people were, Mary Lee thought, as if life and death were much the same; only a quiet step between farm or cottage and this sunny, peaceful spot. She wandered among the headstones, reading a name here and there. Hay-Sweet was one, most appropriate to its surroundings. Knights, Badcocks and Dinwiddys, Vicarys and Chilcotts. It was like meeting old friends; she'd stopped, with Gillian, to talk to people with these same names in cottage doorways and pocket-handkerchief gardens. She often waved good night to their round faced, pink-cheeked children in bedroom windows if she walked down to the duck pond in the evening, and the whole village now smiled and spoke whenever she passed by.

But her thoughts were interrupted by Mr. Clatworthy, who came over to lean on his scythe exactly like Father Time himself.

"My old Granny and Granfer lie in the far corner, Miss," he informed her, waving a somewhat grimy hand. "But I don't rightly know which grave is which. No one can't tell from the stones, so worn they be. I've buried two wives 'ere and there's room for me between 'em when my time comes." He was almost gay about it. "A proper gardener I be," he continued. "You come up to my cottage one afternoon, Miss, and I'll show you the prettiest peas ever you looked at —*and* onions. First prize for onions at all the 'orticulturals in West Zomerzet I've always got and always will."

"I'd like to come very much," said Mary Lee. "Especially if you grow flowers as well. Do you?"

"Can't nobody touch my lupins." Mr. Clatworthy seemed to have the highest opinion of his ability in any direction. "No, nor my roses neither; not at Zomer'aze nor Cary Court nor nowheres else. Mrs. Randall, she likes 'er garden a bit wild, like. Common posies, she'll 'ave, boy's love and London pride and mind-your-own-business that'll spread all over just like a weed."

"But what lovely names!" exclaimed Mary Lee. "And what do you call that gorgeous pink blossom growing on the wall over there?"

"Kiss-me-quick," he replied, giving the flowers an unfriendly glance. "Very common, that is. There's some calls it Valerien and my old mother, she would 'ave it it was Taunton drunkards, but kiss-me-quick is its proper name."

Mrs. Randall emerged from the church just then and carried her rosemary to her husband's grave. She stood looking down for a moment. Afterwards she joined Mary Lee and Mr. Clatworthy and made a few suggestions to the old man about his work.

"Not that it'll do the least good," she said, as they took their homeward way. "But it saves the Vicar from arguing with him. Mr. Clatworthy is the stubbornest soul in the village and that's saying a lot. Wouldn't have electricity wired to his cottage—it's dangerous according to him. I promised Mr. Aldrich I'd speak to him about that awful bed of nettles in the southwest corner, but Mr. Clatworthy says they've always been there and he 'don't 'old with change.'

"Have you got into nettles yet, child?"

Mary Lee said she hadn't.

"You will do," Mrs. Randall assured her. "And they can give you a nasty sting, so be careful if you go out in socks, won't you?"

There was to be a garden party fête for the benefit of the church on the vicarage lawn in mid-June while the roses were at their height.

Because she was handy with a paint-box, Rose

had been selected to make posters, and these appeared at the bus stop, the Heart-in-Hand, the window of the shop and on a conspicuous shed door which was used for announcements of all sorts.

Mrs. Randall prowled about the house picking out articles for the "white elephant" stand.

"Not that there's much left," she said, "after all the 'bring and buy' sales we've had, but one must contribute something. This will be quite a do. Lady Cary is coming over to open it; a title helps a bit, I think, even in these days."

Mary Lee, overhearing, sought Gillian.

"Is—is Lady Cary the one who lives at Cary Court?" she asked. "The place where you went to school?"

"Right. We call her our Auntie Madge. We're hardly related at all really—not since Chloe's time—but we've always been great friends so we still pretend to be cousins."

"Yes. Jeff said so. But what I really wanted to ask about was titles, because we don't have them in America, you know, and Mother thinks it's important to get people's names right. I just say 'Lady Cary,' don't I? If I meet her at the fête, I mean."

"Of course. And her husband is Sir Christopher—he's a baronet," Gillian explained. "He won't be at this thing but some of the others may. I know Dick and Sylvia are down for their half-term break. It's too utterly horrid that Jeff couldn't get home, isn't it?"

One of the nicest things about Gill was her open affection for her brother.

Mary Lee hoped—but thought it hardly likely—that Lady Cary might open the fête wearing a floor-length dress, a glittering coronet and corsage of orchids.

For several minutes it did not occur to her that the slight little woman standing beside Mr. Aldrich on the vicarage steps was Lady Cary. Why, her summer suit was not nearly so smart as Mom's, and her handbag was almost shabby. There were no orchids. Instead, a small pig-tailed girl from the village was thrust forward to present her with a bunch of pink roses. It was then that Mary Lee noticed how reassuringly Lady Cary smiled at the child, who was shy to the brink of tears, how delightfully her eyes crinkled at the corners as she did so.

The Vicar made a short prayer for a successful afternoon, Lady Cary followed with a few words about the needs of the church, thanked the listening group of people for coming and declared the fête open. That was all there was to it.

"I do think she ought to have waved a wand or cut a ribbon, or something," Mary Lee whispered to Gillian, remembering pictures she'd seen in newspapers.

"Oh, I don't believe Auntie Madge would be much good at waving a wand," Gillian said, laughing. "You're thinking of fairy godmothers, aren't you? Now, how about nipping around the stalls to see if there's anything we want before the crowd gets any bigger, Mary Lee?"

They nipped.

Each of the children had been supplied with ten shillings to spend at the fête.

Pat straightway spent sixpence for a garishly pretty blue and pink jug which was to be a present for Nannie. He then headed for a popular table with a sign on it saying Lucky Dip, where he ran into his sister and Gillian.

"Same thing as a grab bag," Pat announced, after a quick glance. "I wonder why they don't learn the right names for things over here? And they've got the queerest money. Look, Mary Lee, what's this?"

He held up a shilling.

Pat, Mary Lee realised suddenly, had had no opportunity to learn about English coins. He had been shut in in London and, at the farm, he had almost no need for money. She took what he had and got it changed into pennies and sixpences. Surely he couldn't go far wrong with these.

They spent some time at the Lucky Dip stall, fishing up the mysterious little tissue-wrapped packages. Pat was delighted with a tiny bottle of very strong scent and ran off to give it to his mother.

"He's the most generous kid in the world, I do believe," Mary Lee said. "Look, Gill, will you swap your china dog for this *awful* brooch with all the jewels on it? I collect china animals."

Gillian examined the glittering brooch.

"I don't like it much," was her comment. "But I'll take it. It will be just the right Christmas present for Mrs. Buffin, don't you think?"

After that they drifted into a field behind the vicarage garden where a number of boards had been laid down to make a temporary bowling alley. To Mary Lee's surprise the game was drawing a larger crowd than anything else at the fête.

"But of course," Gillian said. "It's the last day of Skittle Week. They've been playing every night at the Heart where there's a first-class alley. There are good prizes; didn't you notice on Mummy's posters? 'First prize for men, a Pig—For ladies, a Load of Logs.' Mr. Dinwiddy has probably made a fortune on beer and cider but the church will have done nicely, too, at sixpence for every three throws. Want to have a try?"

Oh yes, Mary Lee would like to, and while they waited their turn, Pat reappeared.

Mary Lee, good-naturedly instructed by several young farm labourers, did very well, bringing down five of the nine wooden pins with one throw.

"What say you, Sam!" exclaimed one of her backers. "The young lady's apt to make a champion, 'ent she?"

"Beginner's luck," said Sam. "Always 'appens so."

The largest ball was so heavy for small Pat that he over-balanced and fell flat on his face when it came to his final throw, but he scrambled to his feet, even more amused than the onlookers who promptly voted him another try, free of charge. This time his effort was so wild that the wooden ball bounded right off the boards, catching Sam a glancing blow on the shin. Pat was quite overwhelmed when he saw his victim hopping from foot to foot and murmured that he was "so sorry," but the crowd seemed to regard it as the funniest incident of the afternoon and roared with laughter.

Mary Lee felt that matters were getting a little out of hand and she and Gillian, between them, hustled her young brother away, still apologising.

They encountered the Vicar, who told them that their party was assembling for tea.

"Is Mr. Aldrich going to that field to skittle?" asked Mary Lee.

Gillian nodded. "He's frightfully good at it," she said. "It wouldn't surprise me if he won the pig."

Two tables had been pushed together and Carys and Randalls were gathered round them when the children reached the lawn.

Casual introductions took place, but Mary Lee found it all a little confusing. She confided as much to a tall, pretty girl, several years her senior, whom she found beside her at the table.

"The trick is not to try to sort us all out at once," the girl told her, laughing. "I'm Sylvia and that's my brother Dick next your mother. We're the oldest grandchildren and we've just got here. The little fat girl is Bobbles Bentley, one of our many cousins. She came with Granny whom you've just met. Now isn't that simple? You'll meet more of us before the summer's over, I dare say—I hear you're staying at Somerhaze until September. So nice for dear little Gill—she must bring you to the Court often, for tennis and things."

Mary Lee thanked her for the invitation. She was charmed with Sylvia, who had helped her through what might have been an awkward moment.

She glanced across the table at Dick, in animated conversation with her mother. He was good-looking, his manner as easy and attractive as his sister's, and she felt a sudden shy longing for his notice and approval.

Sylvia, aware of the glance, laughed again. "Dick," she warned, "will charm you off your feet. I shouldn't let him if I were you. He's a bit cockier than usual to-day because he's just got through a rather sticky set of exams. For his Oxford college. He'll have to do his National Service before he goes up, poor lamb. Do you ride, by the way, Mary Lee?"

"Yes. Not as well as Gill does, of course, but I love it."

"Then you'll see quite a lot of my brother. He rides with young Gill fairly often when he's here."

Sylvia turned to exchange family news with Rose.

And Mary Lee overheard Dick inviting her mother to come and see the gazebo!

"You will appreciate the place," he said, with a flattering accent on the word "you." "When your husband comes down you must bring him over to have tea with me there. It's very, very Regency, you know."

Mrs. Wade smiled and accepted the invitation.

Her daughter breathed a small envious sigh.

Then suddenly, everyone's attention was centred on Gillian.

"And what," Gillian was asking intensely, "what will you do with Bobbles' pony while she's away? I'll board it free for August, Auntie Madge, if you'll let me have it. Will you?"

It seemed that Lady Cary had been telling Mrs. Randall that Bobbles' mother was planning to take her children to France for a month during the summer holiday.

"But, Gill dear," Rose protested, "that pony is a little bit of a thing. Why ever do you want it?"

"Because," Dick cut in teasingly, "our Gillyflower simply can't resist adding another pony to her string—that's all."

Gillian's colour rose and there was an ominous spark in her eye, but she ignored Dick and answered her mother's question.

"I want it for Pat. I want *awfully* to have him ride at the Wiveliscombe Show. He's only eight and he'd have to have something under 12-2 hands to get into the young classes. I've been thinking about it a lot lately. Oh, Mummy, Pat's riding has come on so well—he's really good now."

Dick shifted sides without a moment's hesitation.

"The pony's eating its head off in pasture and Bobbles would love you to have it," he said. "I'll bring the little brute over myself, on the first of August. Right, Bobbles?"

The small, plump girl looked up, nodded affably, and applied herself again to a large bowl of strawberries and cream.

Gillian beamed on both her cousins.

Pat showed his approval of the scheme by giving Gill a hearty thump and grinning broadly.

The crowd was thinning out. Mrs. Randall urged the Carys to come back to the farm. "I've bought no less than *three* cakes," she said. "Two on purpose, and the third because I was afraid Mrs. Canditt was going to have it left at her stall. The children can play a round game, or something, and then we'll have a latish supper."

It was a wonderful evening; Mary Lee thought she had never had more fun. Being at an age when she divided people into two categories only, the grown-ups and the non-grown-ups, she could not decide in which to place Dick and Sylvia. But, of their own volition, they joined the "children" (Dick proclaiming that he and Pat must stick together in such a bevy of women) and played Happy Families with much noise and good-natured bickering, seeming to enjoy the silly game as much as anyone.

After the Carys' departure, a very sleepy Bobbles in the little two-seater car with her grandmother, and Dick and Sylvia walking home by the foot-path through the fields, Mary Lee said good night and went upstairs.

Without turning on the light in her room, she leaned for a few minutes in the open casement window. There was a scent of lilacs in the air, and moonlight blended with twilight, for the summer days were at their longest now. It would never be dark at all to-night. She could dimly see the flower clusters on the big chestnut tree and, far away across the pasture, a flicker of white which might, or might not, be the lacy woollen stole that Sylvia had thrown about her shoulders this evening.

11. *Gill's Birthday*

NOW THAT THE children were completely at home on the farm, Mrs. Wade often joined her husband for several days at a time. He continued his week-ends at Somerhaze when work permitted.

Mary Lee had early been shown a small panelled library beyond the dining-room and made free of the many books there. Kipling's *Puck of Pook's Hill* and *Rewards and Fairies* were among her discoveries. When she told her father she was reading Jane Austen, he took her to Bath for two wonderful days.

Mary Lee was riding Skittles regularly now, since Bramble was the more appropriate pony for Pat.

Gill, of course, rode the Connemara mare—Colleen.

Mary Lee growing ever more ambitious, wanted to try Colleen herself, but Gillian wouldn't hear of it.

"She's better broken than I expected from what the Major said," she admitted. "But, if she should happen to put you off, it would undo a lot of my work with her, I'm afraid."

"And what about me if she 'put me off?'" asked Mary Lee with a pretence of indignation. "I suppose it wouldn't matter a bit if my neck got broken!"

"Oh, a tumble in the paddock wouldn't hurt you," Gill assured her with an elfish grin. "But I'm not at all keen about Colleen trying any tricks with me at a show when Major Adcock might be watching us. I'm lucky, lucky, lucky," and she spun on her toes, as was her way when happiest, "to have this pony, because she's just right for the classes I'll be in at Wiveliscombe. I'll be thirteen before then."

"You mean you're having a birthday? Oh, when, Gill?"

"On the thirteenth. Where are you off to, Mary Lee? Mary Le-e-e!"

Mary Lee was off to the house to find her mother and consult her about Gill's birthday.

"And what about presents, Mom?" she asked, after a breathless announcement of the situation. "We haven't much time and I'd love to do something really *big* for Gill: she—well, all the Randalls—are giving us such a wonderful summer, aren't they?"

"They are," her mother agreed. "They treat us like invited guests instead of P.G's. Gillian's birthday offers us a chance to show our appreciation tactfully. Rose would never refuse the child what I have in mind for her, but she and I had better talk it over first, I think."

Her talk with Rosemary resulted in an invitation for the two girls to spend the following Saturday with Mrs. Wade at Minehead. The day, she said, would include a surprise, but even Mary Lee did not know what it was all about until her mother led them into a small, select shop that displayed riding clothes in the window.

Gillian was overwhelmed when she learned that her birthday gift from the Wades was to be an entire new outfit.

"But—but—Mrs. Wade," she stammered, "I really don't need a coat. I just ride in a shirt and jodhpurs at the summer gymkhanas."

"And aren't you riding that Irish pony at a couple of shows this fall?"

Gill nodded, speechless.

"Well, then." The jacket was tried on, and it fitted without need of alteration.

"I—I—just don't know how to thank you," Gillian said at last. "Sylvia gave me the things I've been wearing, old ones of hers, but I've almost outgrown them and they're getting awfully shabby, besides."

Mrs. Wade smiled. "It doesn't half make up for all the coaching you've given the children," she said. "And now, if you will, you can help me select some jodhpurs for Mary Lee; those frontier pants look all wrong in this country. And for Pat—I have his measurements with me. He simply can't appear at a show in shorts."

Gillian was quick to admit that he couldn't.

Later they had tea, and Mrs. Wade kept Gill talking while Mary Lee slipped away to do a bit of shopping by herself. Pat had produced some money that morning and asked her to get "something pretty " for him to give Gillian. So she was carrying two small packages, which she tried to keep out of sight, when she met the others at the bus station. She need not have worried; Gill was unaware of anything but the big suit-box hugged in her own arms.

She insisted on wearing her new riding things at her birthday tea.

"And I don't blame her at all," Rose said, laughing. "It's the best-looking outfit I ever saw, and frankly, the child's legs are meant for jodhpurs; she's growing so fast she looks skinny in dresses just now."

There was a cake with candles. Gillian's face got pinker and pinker as she blew them out and turned to open her little pile of gifts.

Mary Lee had chosen well: a small silk scarf

the colour of ripe corn, with a design of foxes' masks in Gill's favourite blue; and, for Pat's present, yellow string gloves.

Rose had made a dress for her daughter—white piqué, very plain, with a wide, blue, suede belt, which everyone agreed would become her.

Jeff had remembered the date and sent her a short necklet of simple white china beads.

But Mrs. Randall's gift was, perhaps, the most exciting of all. She brought in the old bone-handled crop with a silver band bearing her maiden initials that she had cherished since her hunting days.

Tears were on Gillian's lashes as she thanked her with a kiss.

"I took the thong off, my sweet," Mrs. Randall said, "because you don't hunt. I whipped in for the Master for two seasons, you know, when Sir Christopher had the hounds. It's still a bond between us." She went on to tell of meets at the Court and by their own duck pond or in front of the Heart-in-Hand—of runs across country, every mile of which she remembered.

"You almost make me want to hunt, Gran," Gillian said at last. "You know I've ridden ponies to meets, just to get them used to it, and I've hated to turn back when the hounds moved off but—but—I don't think I could bear to kill things."

"It's a matter for each to decide," her grandmother said with a sigh. "I couldn't now. All life seems to have become more precious since the war—even a fox's."

There was a short, poignant silence. Rose broke it.

"I don't want to sound heartless," she said flatly, "but I could have cheerfully murdered the little red thief-of-the-world that butchered my best Aylesbury ducks last winter. So there!"

The statement, from gentle Rosemary, set them all laughing.

The birthday festivities were soon followed by the long-looked-forward-to breaking up of school, first Gill's, then Jeffrey's.

It was good to have Jeff home again. The hay-making and the cows claimed much of his time, for he did his share of the evening milking, but the young people were all in a holiday mood.

Mary Lee found that none of them was too old to enjoy the mangel house, which now boasted matting on the hard earthen floor, several old garden chairs and a battered table. They even rigged a cowbell outside the door—much to Pat's satisfaction—which any adult was requested to ring before entering.

The day came when Bramble and Skittles were claimed by their owners, two nice enough girls, Mary Lee admitted, though she was critical of their riding. She and Gillian were sitting glumly on the paddock fence—they had been sitting there ever since the departure of the ponies.

"Those girls are out of practice," Gill said fairly. "And the awful thing is that that could happen to Pat. *You're* all right, you can use Posy, but she's miles too big for him. So's Mousie, besides being slower than a slug. Of course, a few days without riding won't hurt Pat, but he doesn't know a thing about the relay race yet. Oh dear, I suppose I'll just have to go to the Court and ask for Tuppence."

"Tuppence?"

"That's the Exmoor pony. Bobbles' pony."

"Oh! Wasn't . . . didn't . . ." Mary Lee spoke very casually indeed. "Didn't your cousin say something about bringing the pony over?"

"Dick? He did. But you don't know Dick if you believe he'll ever think of it again."

"Maybe he hasn't come down yet." Mary Lee felt impelled to make the suggestion, though it was no business of hers to defend Dick Cary.

"Oh yes he has. Auntie Madge has got a houseful of her grandchildren there. She phoned Mummy this morning to ask if we'd come over to-morrow for tea and tennis. Well, maybe I can ask about Tuppence then."

As Gill finished speaking, Mary Lee looked up. Dick was riding towards them on a big chestnut horse. The small, shaggy creature trotting alongside was obviously Tuppence.

"There!" Mary Lee said in triumph. "You see!"

She was pleasantly aware of the fact that she was wearing her new jodhpurs.

Gill had on her old ones, and there was a three-cornered tear in the shoulder of her blue cotton shirt. But she was completely unselfconscious, her eyes on the chestnut horse.

"Hallo!" Dick hailed them.

"Where did you get him?" asked Gillian.

"In case you don't remember," Dick explained, "it's Bobbles' pony. Name of Tuppence. And I got him out of a five-acre pasture where I've been chasing him for the last hour or two."

"Of course I know Tuppence," Gill said impatiently. "I mean that chestnut. Don't tell me he's yours?"

"Alas, no. I'm merely keeping him for a friend. If my little cousin can board horses, why not I? He's a young thing and skittish. I wish you'd take this pony away before he gets a kick in the ribs. I've been frightened to death it would happen all the way over here—not but what Tuppence deserves it, the little demon! When a motor-bike passed us I thought we were for it; Jester and I were jammed against the hedge on one side of the road and Tuppence sitting in the ditch on the other."

Gillian laughed shortly. "You could have led Tuppence across the fields with less trouble," she said. "But I suppose you wanted to show off that horse. You wouldn't let me up on him, would you? Just here in the paddock?"

"I would not. I value your life too highly, my pet. What I thought was that you and I might have a little school, if you'd throw a saddle on your grey mare. And over the very mildest of jumps, mind! Something that will tumble if one so much as touches it."

For the next hour Gillian was Dick's willing slave. She hauled poles about, raising or lowering jumps. She put Posy over them to give Jester a lead, or followed after if Dick preferred it.

Mary Lee, too, was pressed into service. First she was sent scurrying to shut the ever-present dogs in the barn. She was requested to sit on the fence holding Tuppence and Colleen by their halters to keep them out of the way.

Dick was, suddenly, a different person—serious, careful, patient when the young horse made a mistake. He was appreciative, too, of Gillian's help. Mary Lee had been aware of the bickering between these two; now they worked in perfect accord, their interests one.

Lucky, lucky Gill, she thought, and was pleased when Jeff appeared from nowhere to join her.

"This," he remarked, perching beside her on the rails, "will make Gill's day. The mare's going well, isn't she? A lot better than that animal of Dick's." He laughed as Jester cleared one jump at twice its height and stopped abruptly at the next with his nose on the top bar

"Perhaps Gill's a better rider," Mary Lee suggested, though reluctantly.

"Don't you believe it," Jeff told her. "Dick's one of the best for miles around. It's the ambition of Gill's life to catch up with him. She gets more practice, but he's older and has good judgment. He'll bring that young horse out now before it goes sour on him. You'll see. Gill would keep it up all morning."

Jeff was right. One more round and the two riders walked their horses over to the fence, Gill with a happy smile on her flushed face.

She invited her cousin to lunch at Somerhaze. He could rub the chestnut down and put him in the stable to cool off. But Dick refused. He said he'd prefer to keep Jester moving.

Or was he fearful of being bored by his young companions, Mary Lee wondered?

"Sylly told me you'd all be over for tennis to-morrow," he said. "I may see you then. And we'll have another go here with the horses, Gill, my sweet, before long. You and the mare were very useful this morning, I must say. Thanks a lot."

"And thank *you*, Dick, for bringing the pony over," Gillian responded. "I enjoyed our ride so much."

"So did I," Dick called back over his shoulder, as he and Jester moved at a sedate pace towards the yard gate.

Jeffrey had run ahead to open it for him.

"Just look at that," Gillian said. "When Dick Cary turns on the charm, everyone rushes about doing whatever he wants at the moment. Not me, though—he needn't think he can twist me round his little finger."

Nor could she understand why Mary Lee went off in a gale of laughter.

12. *Mr. Ballardy*

PAT AND TUPPENCE went together like a song, according to Gillian.

"The pony's been out at grass too long," she said. "But Pat and I will soon get him into shape. And do you know what? I met Mr. Aldrich at the shop this morning and he told me his grandson is coming to spend part of the holidays at the vicarage. Oh, a horrid little boy he is—not that the Vicar thinks so—but they've got hold of a pony for him and he'll ride with us."

"Where's the advantage in that?" Jeff asked. "He's a disgusting child, if he's the one I'm thinking of—Wilfred, by name?"

"That's him," Gill acknowledged with fine

disregard for grammar. "The advantage is, Jeff, that he'll give Pat some competition, which will do him a world of good."

Meanwhile Mary Lee and Jeffrey, who took their riding less seriously than Gillian, went wandering off over the hills, he on the grey mare and she on old Mousie.

She loved such unhurried rambles. Wild foxgloves were in bloom at the edges of woodlands, forget-me-nots by the streams; the hilltops were purple-pink with heather and ling and the corn in the fields pale gold.

Sometimes all four children rode up Butterfly Combe to one of the little glades, taking sandwiches and picnicking there.

It was at the end of one of these expeditions that they kidnapped Mr. Ballardy—or so Mrs. Randall put it sometime later.

Mary Lee glanced over the wall into the garden of the Heart-in-Hand as they rode home at a footpace. It looked very inviting with the sunshine slanting across, and the purple clematis in full bloom over the inn door. All the wooden tables but one were unoccupied. She remembered what Gillian had once told her about strawberry teas.

"Is it too late for strawberries?" she asked, pulling Mousie to a halt. Old Mouse could move briskly enough when she was this near home.

Jeff caught the idea at once.

"It's not too late for raspberries anyway," he

said. "Not to mention cut-rounds with jam and cream. I'm starving. Has anyone got any money? I haven't."

"Oh, Mrs. Dinwiddy will do it on tick." Gill was already turning Colleen. "Do let's. We can tie the horses in the yard."

"I thought of it, so it's my treat," Mary Lee announced grandly. "I'll run up and pay for it this evening."

Tea was a lavish affair and time did not matter at all, since Jeff had agreed to forgo the milking for once.

The first pangs of hunger satisfied, they became mildly interested in the elderly gentleman sitting alone in the far corner. He wore old-fashioned golfing plus-fours and woollen socks. Grizzled hair and exceptionally heavy eye-brows gave him a severe expression, but he smiled at the children in quite a friendly way when their eyes met his.

"Not local," Jeff murmured to his sister.

"Never saw him before," Gill whispered back.

They returned the smile.

He lit a pipe and strolled over to their table.

"May I join you for a few minutes?" he asked pleasantly. "You live in the vicinity, I imagine; a lovely part of the world. I was down here on a bicycling tour many years ago and thought I should like to see it again in a more leisurely way. But accommodation is scarce."

"Is the Heart full up, sir?" Jeff asked.

"Yes, unfortunately. There are only four rooms for guests and they're all taken."

"It's the beginning of the tourist season," Gill announced with a sigh. "We aren't bothered much in the village because we're half a mile from the main road. The only motor buses are for Mother's Outings or the Women's Institute. And we have an occasional artist or something."

"I should think you well might attract artists. I explored the village before tea."

"Have you tried the Cary Arms at Stogary?" Jeff asked.

"No. Because I've quite set my heart on Midsomer-St. Mary. I've got a small, ancient car and expect to drive round a good deal, but I'd like to make this my centre. You don't know any cottage people who'd take a paying guest, I suppose?"

"Only Nannie—Mrs. Chilcott, that is; and she won't take anybody but children. She's keeping two small ones for somebody now, and you know how they can yell."

The gentleman rejected this idea promptly and firmly.

They thought about the problem in silence for a moment. Pat broke it.

"He could sleep in the old schoolroom," he suggested. "We aren't using it for anything since the holidays began, are we?"

"He doesn't like children, Pat," Mary Lee reminded him in a low voice.

"Well, I'm the youngest and he can decide about me now," Pat declared stoutly.

"There are two sides to the question," their new acquaintance said with a chuckle. "The children might not like me. Though I've managed to co-exist with vast numbers of boys for thirty years, due to the fact that I've been Senior Classical Master at a boys' school."

He named it and Jeffrey was impressed.

"Golly, sir," he breathed respectfully. "I'd think you'd find us mild after that."

"Ballardy is my name," they were told now. "I assume that there are some adults in your establishment? Good! If you think there's the least chance that they might find me acceptable, I'll present myself at once."

"We can but try, sir," Jeff said with a friendly grin.

So Mr. Ballardy was added to the household.

"Of course, we never dreamed of taking anyone else this summer," Mrs. Randall explained to Mrs. Wade. "And we won't, unless you approve, but the children laid him on the doorstep just like a cat bringing in a mouse and he so wants to stay. He'd have the old bath, of course, because it's right next the schoolroom, and he says it's just the sort he's been used to. I don't think he'll be troublesome at all."

Far from being troublesome, Mr. Ballardy fitted in nicely.

The first Sunday that he accompanied the

Randalls to a church service it was discovered that he had a pleasing baritone voice. Musical evenings at Somerhaze became frequent, often with the addition of guests from the vicarage or Cary Court.

One evening Jeffrey succumbed to his grandmother's pleading for a solo.

"You know my voice is apt to crack up at any moment now, Gran," he said beforehand, "but they keep risking my three-fold solo 'Amen' in school chapel, so I'll have a try at 'Oh, for the Wings of a Dove,' if you really want me to."

Jeff's voice didn't crack; it soared, pure and very true.

And Mary Lee knew she would always remember the lovely room as it was then: the group of friends, old and young; Jeff's voice; the soft evening light beyond the great bay window. Her throat tightened and she felt the prick of tears behind her eyelids. It would be dreadful—unthinkable—if she were to cry. Jeff had once told her proudly that Gillian *never* cried. She turned and saw Dick looking directly at her, his eyebrows raised, his mouth quirked up at one corner. Deliberately, he winked. Mary Lee swallowed, blinked her lashes and sent him a wavering, grateful smile. It was the first time he'd ever been really aware of her, she thought.

Dick's awareness was not sufficient to include Mary Lee in the invitation to her parents for tea at the gazebo. Afterwards they were taken through the Palladian mansion by Sir Christopher and Lady Cary.

Mary Lee had tea on the little lawn at the gatehouse with a bewildering number of young people. Later they played tennis.

"That's just one of the advantages of having the place a school now," Sylvia said. "They keep the tennis courts in prime condition. And Granny is allowed to sleep some of us in the mistresses' rooms during the summer holiday. We'd be too much of a squash at the gatehouse."

Naturally the conversation was of Cary Court that evening at suppertime.

"I wish you might have seen it when the family was in residence," Mrs. Randall said to Mr. Wade. "As a school it's bound to appear empty. Properly furnished, it was a very handsome home."

"I can well believe it. But I suppose the Carys can count themselves fortunate to have let it so well. And you're even more fortunate to live in a charming house that's manageable and still a home."

"A perfect house," murmured Mr. Ballardy, rather unexpectedly. "And hospitable. It lacks only one detail."

"What's that?" queried his hostess. "Perhaps we can supply it."

"A ghost."

Mary Lee told Gillian later that she almost giggled when she heard these words. Surely Mr. Ballardy was joking. It seemed to her completely out of keeping with the scholarly gentleman they knew.

She was wrong. Mr. Ballardy took the subject of ghosts (Paranormal Phenomena was the elaborate term he used) quite seriously. He corresponded with people of a like interest and had written several articles for publications that dealt with such matters.

So he was both pleased and excited to hear the story of the Somerhaze ghost, which Mrs. Randall told him at once and in full.

"How delightful! How truly delightful!" He repeated it again and again. "And how strange it is that these apparitions seem to concern themselves with trivial matters, as in this case—merely the name of a race horse. It's quite beyond our comprehension, isn't it?"

He spent much time, after this, studying Chloe's portrait.

The children, since they had originally introduced Mr. Ballardy to the household, regarded him as their protegé. They felt a degree of responsibility for his entertainment and well-being. They discussed this new aspect of the man when they met for "elevenses" in the mangel house next morning, as had become their custom.

"Well, his interest in this thing doesn't surprise me in the least," Jeff announced.

"But, Jeff, he's really a highbrow," Mary Lee protested. "How can he? . . ."

Jeff interrupted her.

"That's just it. These scholarly blokes like to keep what they call an open mind on all subjects, including the supernatural. One of our masters at school is just the same. But he's a Merton man and it's well known that Merton College has a very troublesome ghost. They have to get it exorcised by a parson every seven years or so, I believe."

Mary Lee stared at Jeff, speechless.

But Gillian said cheerfully, "Oh, well, from all we've heard, Chloe sounds a friendly enough soul. And it doesn't matter to us if Mr. Ballardy is a bit on the dotty side; he's a good sort and I hope he sticks around a while, myself."

"You said it," agreed Jeff, who enjoyed using what he considered Americanisms for Mary Lee's benefit. "Let alone the fact that he's giving me an hour's coaching in Latin every day. He suggested it when I told him it was my weakest subject. It keeps the old boy's hand in. He's retired now, you know, and a bit at a loose end, I should think."

Pat, bored with the discussion, had left the mangel house ten minutes ago and had wandered off.

"He's gone down to meet Wilfred in the paddock," Gill said. "I'm giving those kids a good workout this morning."

Jeff and Mary Lee decided to stroll along and watch.

"It won't be Gill's fault if Pat doesn't win an

event or two at Wiveliscombe," he observed when they were comfortably established on the fence a few minutes later. "That is, provided he survives her coaching methods."

Potatoes had been placed on top of poles driven into the ground at suitable intervals. The boys were galloping across the paddock, plucking the potatoes off, hurling them into waiting baskets on the other side of the field, and repeating the performance.

Mary Lee laughed lazily at Jeff's comment.

"Oh, he'll survive," she said. "As a matter of fact, I've never seen Pat looking so well. Mom and Dad are always talking about it—and gloating."

"Golly!" exclaimed Jeff at that moment. "Look at Tuppence go! I'd never have supposed he had such a turn of speed in him!"

"Gill expects it of him," Mary Lee said. "And what Gill expects she gets, whether it's from Pat or the pony, if you've noticed. She even had me doing pretty well when Bramble was here."

Jeffrey gave her a quick glance.

"You ride Posy very nicely. But she's ineligible for a pony class, and open events at these gymkhanas are mostly for jumping. Fairly stiff jumps, too. I'm afraid you'd hardly be up to it yet."

"Oh, no." Mary Lee still sounded a little wistful. If Bramble and Skittles had remained at the farm she might have been competing in the coming show along with Pat and Gillian.

"Well, if you ask me, I think you and I are in luck. If we had anything suitable to ride Gill'd have us out there now working our heads off."

But Jeff had spoken too soon.

Pat rode up to the fence only a minute afterwards to say that Gill needed him.

"She wants us to practise for the relay," Pat said. "And Toad's pony won't stand still for the start. It goes backward and he can't stop it."

"Toad?"

"Yes. Wilfred. He doesn't want to be called Wilfred any more, though. He says the kids at school call him Toad, so I do too."

"A step in the right direction, certainly," Jeff commented, sliding off the fence. "So I'll oblige by holding Toad's pony for him. Much better than shoving from the rear. Safer, too. Does the animal have a name, by the way?"

"Her name's Judy. She's a mare," Pat said, grinning. He was easily amused these days.

Jeff sauntered across the field, hands in pockets.

Gillian was now mounted on Colleen, a short stick in her hand, and explaining to Wilfred (or Toad) how to proceed. She, at the word "Go!" pronounced by Jeffrey, would race once round the field; he, Toad (or Wilfred) would be waiting, would grasp the stick the instant she reached him and gallop round the field in his turn, as fast as Judy could set hoof to the ground.

Toad may have understood these orders; Judy did not. The minute Colleen leapt forward she tried to follow. When Toad got her stopped, she began to back. Jeff caught her rein, and she continued to back. Then things happened rapidly.

Toad let go the rein and a short tug of war took place between Jeff and the pony. Judy sat down and Toad rolled off; the throat-latch gave way; Judy went over backwards, and Jeff was left standing with the bridle in his hand just as Gill swept up prepared to hand Toad the stick.

Mary Lee watched only long enough to see Toad and the pony scramble to their feet unhurt, then laughed so much that she fell off the fence.

When she looked again at the figures in the paddock, Jeff, Pat and (be it said to his credit) Toad were doing the same.

"She said—she said——" Jeff gasped, as he staggered over to Mary Lee and leaned on the fence, "Gill said I ought to have hit the fool pony from behind. I couldn't get behind her, she was backing so fast. Oh, golly! Oh, gosh! It was funny, wasn't it? I'm in disgrace all right. And just listen to this, Mary Lee—she expects you to come in there and help now. . . ."

"Oh, I couldn't!" Mary Lee protested, beginning to laugh again. "It was too, too funny!"

So they went away together to laugh it out in the mangel house, leaving Gill to cope with her young riders and their ponies single-handed.

13. *Chloe Walks*

A FEW DAYS later Mary Lee was to look back on that sunny hour in the paddock and wonder how she and Jeff could have been so lighthearted.

Her parents left for a week in Edinburgh the same day and she waved good-bye without a care in the world.

Long afterwards, she heard Jeff refer to the event which took place in their absence as "a spot of bother." At the time it seemed a great deal more than that!

She, Jeff and Gillian were all involved in it. And Mr. Ballardy. Mr. Ballardy was the cause of it, so to speak.

To begin with, he went up to London for a couple of days and Jeff immediately called for a conference of three in the mangel house.

"It's about Mr. B.," he told the girls. "The poor old boy is broody—distinctly broody, I'd say."

Gill looked thoughtful.

"He was clicking away happily enough on his typewriter yesterday," she said. "And, when I took his tea up this morning, he thanked me the way he always does, but now I think of it, he hasn't had much to say lately. Oh, Jeff, you don't suppose he's getting bored, do you?"

"That's what I'm afraid of. And if he's really fed up, he might quite easily do a bunk. I had other plans for him."

"Other plans?" echoed Mary Lee.

"Yes. I've thought a lot about our Mr. B. He's a good type of P.G. They can be stinkers, you know."

"Oh! . . . Not us!" Mary Lee's distress was apparent.

Jeff stared at her; Gill reached over and took her hand.

"Don't be more of a goose than you have to, Mary Lee," the boy advised. "We don't even think of you Wades as P.G's now—you belong at Somerhaze."

The words warmed Mary Lee's heart, as did Gillian's gesture, for Gill was seldom demonstrative, except with animals.

Jeff returned to the original subject. "Yes, I'd made plans for Mr. Ballardy, and for his own good, too. I happen to know, from what he's let fall now and then, that he's without a headquarters since his retirement. I decided he might just as well stay on here—through the autumn and winter anyway. He's not much trouble for Mum and Gran; it's rather nice for them to have a man in the house; and besides . . . Well, what he pays would go a long way towards the new roof by next spring, wouldn't it? He seemed contented enough, too, until lately."

Gill sat with her chin in her hands, frowning. "As I see it," she said, "what Mr. Ballardy wants is something new to be interested in. He's done all these Roman tiles and ruined Abbeys around here."

"He's awfully interested in ghosts." Mary Lee tossed it off carelessly.

There was a moment's silence. Then Jeff hit the table a whack that made both girls jump.

"Chloe!" he exclaimed. "Mary Lee, you're a genius. I'll never call you a goose again!"

"Chloe?"

"Chloe! We'll materialise Chloe for him!"

"Who's being a goose now, Jeff Randall?" his sister asked. "You can't whistle up a ghost the way you would a dog."

"I can whistle up a pretty good imitation. You."

"Me?"

Mary Lee was catching Jeff's excitement. "Of course!" she joined in. "I see what he means, and it'll be the easiest thing in the world, Gill. You—dressed up in that old costume your grandmother told us about. You'll look exactly like the portrait. Mr. Ballardy is bound to fall for it, believing in ghosts the way he does. What fun! Oh, do let's!"

Gill was very quiet, thinking it over.

"I suppose I could do it," she said finally. "It'll have to be me because I am a bit like Chloe—even I can see that."

"Good girl!" Jeff patted her knee approvingly. "Now we'll work out ways and means; we can't afford any mistakes. No one is to know a thing about it but us; like international spy work—the fewer involved, the safer we'll be."

The next quarter of an hour was devoted to planning.

Mary Lee volunteered to ask Mrs. Randall to show her the costume that afternoon, but this, they decided would not do at all. Mr. Ballardy almost certainly would mention Chloe's visitation, and if everyone knew the girls had had the dress a day or two before, the fat would be in the fire.

"But I can't just go into the box-room and pinch it, Jeff," Gillian protested.

"It isn't pinching, it's borrowing," Jeff explained patiently. "And in a good cause, too. You'd better do it now, what's more, because the Vicar and Mrs. Aldrich are coming to lunch and

Mum and Gran will be busy in the kitchen and never give you a thought."

"Where I ought to be helping them this minute," Gill told him.

"Let Mary Lee do it. The first step is for you to get hold of that dress."

The girls departed hastily, Mary Lee to the kitchen and Gillian in the direction of the box-room.

An hour later Mary Lee entered her own bedroom.

Gillian turned from the long looking-glass which hung on the door of the old wardrobe.

Rich ivory-coloured satin hugged her waist closely and fell in heavy folds to the floor; great puffed sleeves covered her thin young arms; the jewelled necklace glittered at her throat and pale curls framed her pink face.

It was as if Chloe—a younger Chloe, but so like—had stepped out of her gold frame.

"Gill!" Mary Lee exclaimed with indrawn breath. "You're beautiful."

Gillian's cheeks turned even rosier at the spontaneous compliment, but she giggled.

"I feel half-naked. Did you ever see such a low neck? My undies show. You'll have to take a tack in the thing, Mary Lee, or put some padding down the top. I'm as tall as Gran, but the skirt seems awfully long. I don't want to fall over it, you know, and I can't wear the slippers—they've got high heels."

"Don't move!" Mary Lee ordered, and dashed for her mother's sewing case.

Adjustments were made, paper tissues thrust down the bodice and a pair of white satin ballet-type bedroom slippers produced.

"I don't dare touch the skirt," Mary Lee said at last. "It isn't much too long; you'll just have to hold it up when you walk. I'm sure ladies did that in Chloe's time. And now I'm going to find Jeff; I want him to see you before you take it off."

Jeff's reaction was one that would have pleased any sister.

"Gill, my girl," he said, after staring at her for a moment, "you ought to wear such things all the time. Well, I suppose you couldn't these days, but when you grow up and go to parties, you simply must. What have you done to your hair?"

"It's a wig."

"Oh. I'm glad you remembered the necklace." He touched it lightly with his fingers. "It's important. Rubies and diamonds, I suppose the stones are meant to be, and tiny, little pearls. A pretty bit of nonsense, if it is a fake."

"There's only one thing lacking." Gill turned again to the mirror, taking the pose of the girl in the portrait, one hand playing with her necklace, the other half-hidden in the folds of the skirt.

"What's that?"

"My little greyhound."

The word "my" gave Mary Lee a queer sensation. Was it Gillian or Chloe whose image gazed back at her from the long glass?

"I don't suppose one of the spaniels would do?" she suggested tentively, and was convinced of Gill's reality by her scornful answer.

"Silly!" said Gillian. "Even a gubbins like old Ballardy must know the difference between a spaniel and a greyhound!"

Mr. Ballardy returned the following evening, but Jeff thought he looked tired.

"Better allow him one good night's sleep," he advised. "When he's seen our Chloe he may stay awake for weeks hoping for another glimpse."

"All right," Gillian agreed. "Only don't let's put it off too long. I'm getting jittery."

"You needn't be. Everything's well in hand. There's a full moon and it'll shine in the old boy's window at just about twelve o'clock. I checked it last night. And you'll only be in his room a minute or two. It isn't as if you had to say anything. Don't panic and bolt out, though —try to float, sort of. I'll wait for you right outside the door, so don't worry."

"All very well for Jeff to say 'don't worry,'" Gillian muttered to Mary Lee as her brother walked away whistling. "He hasn't got to do this 'floating' business, and in a strange man's room at midnight, too."

"Mr. Ballardy isn't a strange man and you've

taken his morning tea up to him ever since he's been here. You're quite used to running in and out of his room," Mary Lee said callously.

"But not floating," Gill reminded her in a small voice.

The next evening the three conspirators watched the full moon rise in a cloudless sky with considerable satisfaction. They bid the family, Mr. Ballardy, and each other a polite good night and went upstairs at the usual time.

Pat had, of course, been in bed for hours. How fortunate, Mary Lee thought, that he slept right down at the end of the corridor, beyond their mother's room which was unoccupied until her return from Scotland.

Gill put on the costume in Mary Lee's room, under her critical eye.

At about eleven o'clock they heard Mr. Ballardy's footsteps pass the door, the roaring of water pipes in the old bathroom, then silence.

Jeff joined them soon afterwards. He was without shoes and insisted that Mary Lee shed hers. "His light's still on," he whispered "We've got to be very, very quiet."

"Is the bathroom door open?" Gill asked. She was to go through the bathroom into Mr. Ballardy's room, hesitate for a moment by the window in the moonlight, and exit by the door into the corridor. The long wait had begun to tell on her nerves and she was shivering.

Jeff nodded. "I opened it," he said. "And I'll be standing by, from the time you go in, to open the other one for you. I'll give you about two minutes. Don't rush it. Mary Lee will wait here and be ready to switch off this light the instant we're back."

"I wish that was now!" Gillian whispered through chattering teeth.

But she pulled herself together and stepped bravely into the passageway when her brother finally reported that Mr. Ballardy's room was dark.

Mary Lee stood at her door, with held breath. They'd been afraid to leave it open more than a crack because of the light, but that would be needed to guide Jeff and Gillian back. It seemed ages before the two slipped into the room as silently as they'd left it. On the instant Mary Lee flicked out the light.

The room seemed pitch-black at first, the moon being on the other side of the house. Soon, however, her eyes adjusted to the darkness, and she could discern Gillian's figure in her pale, shimmering dress.

"How did it go?" Mary Lee barely breathed the question.

"Couldn't have been better!" Jeff gloated. "I got the door open—the least bit and without a sound, mind you—and Gill was standing there in the moonlight, looking like something from another world. . . ."

"I even remembered to smile," Gillian capped his words. "And, when Mr. Ballardy sat up in bed—oh, he sat up all right and took a good look—I did a proper floating act. Didn't I float well, Jeff?"

"You did. I panicked a bit myself then; I was afraid I might not get you away fast enough if the old boy came after us. Golly! What a rag it's been!"

"Did Mr. Ballardy say anything?" Mary Lee asked.

"He said 'Chloe,' I think. As if it were a question, sort of."

They sat in companionable and satisfied silence for a few minutes. Suddenly it was shattered by a long-drawn, high-pitched howl.

Mary Lee hurled herself in the general direction of Gillian, found her and clung to her arm. It was a relief to hear her smothered giggle.

"Frolic," Gill whispered. "It's only Frolic. She does that sometimes, on moonlight nights, the little silly."

"Wh-where is she?" stammered Mary Lee, still clinging. "It s-s-sounded right outside this door."

"Well, it wasn't," Gill assured her soothingly. "She's downstairs in her basket where she always sleeps at night."

Jeff had laughed, too. Now he yawned, declared he was sleepy, said he'd take a final peep down the corridor and go along to bed.

A second later he reported a crack of light showing under Mr. Ballardy's door.

"Reading, to calm his nerves, I dare say," he whispered. "You girls had both better undress in the dark. I mean to. Coming, Gill? Good night, Mary Lee."

Gill and Jeff had been sleeping on the top floor since the house was so full, in what had once been maids' rooms.

They went so quietly that Mary Lee couldn't even hear a stair creak.

She undressed as rapidly as possible, slipped into bed and pulled the covers well up around her ears. In spite of Gillian's perfectly plausible explanation she could not forget that horrid long-drawn howl.

14. *"A Spot of Bother"*

MARY LEE slept fitfully, woke unrefreshed and too late for breakfast in the kitchen with the Randalls.

And, after the beautiful clear moonlit night, it was raining. The window showed tossing tree-tops and dark clouds hanging low.

Gillian came in carrying a cup of tea. Her usually pink face was pale and there were faint blue shadows under her eyes.

"You'd better drink this," she said. "And I might as well tell you—we're for it."

Mary Lee stared at her, appalled.

"About last night, you mean? What went wrong?"

"I lost that beastly necklace. In Mr. Ballardy's room."

"Oh, Gill, you're sure? Couldn't it have slipped off in here? Or in the passageway?"

"No such luck. I missed it when I started to undress. Of course I told Jeff and he came down and searched every inch of the corridor with his little torch. We knew we were all right if it had fallen off in your room and Jeff didn't want to rouse you again to look. Then, when I took tea in to Mr. Ballardy this morning, there the wretched thing was—glittering on his bedside table. I nearly dropped the tray! He didn't say a word about it, nor did I. Oh, it was an awful moment, Mary Lee! I was feeling rotten anyway; I hadn't slept a wink all night, between worrying over the necklace and—and—a perfectly frightful row with Jeff. He—Mary Lee, he practically called me a liar."

Gill collapsed on the foot of the bed and stared, unseeing, at the moving branches beyond the window.

A row between Gill and Jeffrey! Mary Lee had never known them to so much as quarrel before.

"What was it about?" she asked. "He didn't blame you for losing the necklace, did he? Gill, he *couldn't.*"

"Oh, no, he was awfully decent about that. He wouldn't even let me help him look for it because he thought I was tired. No, it was later. He said I'd gone downstairs—right down into the hall—and beckoned him to follow, which he did. Then he couldn't find me anywhere. Now I ask you, Mary Lee, would I be playing hide and seek at two o'clock in the morning? And wearing that long dress? It's the maddest nonsense! When he came up and saw me in bed, in pyjamas, he was furious. Naturally I told him I hadn't left my room at all and that's when he called me a liar. As a matter of fact I've never lied to Jeff in my life—nor to anyone else, much. I don't think I'd be very good at it."

She wouldn't, either, Mary Lee thought, meeting Gillian's honest eyes. But first things must come first; Mr. Ballardy would have to be coped with. To this Gill agreed.

"He's in the dining-room now," she said, "having breakfast with Pat. He's bound to kick up an awful dust, but shall we go down and get it over?"

Mary Lee nodded grimly. Her heart was hammering however, and Gill looked white as a sheet when they entered the dining-room a few minutes later.

The post had come and there was a neat little pile of letters beside Mr. Ballardy's plate. He said good morning and went on slitting envelopes with a silver butter-spreader. It was not until Jeff joined them that he looked up, took off his horn-rimmed glasses and said, pleasantly enough, "We will excuse you now, Patrick, if you've finished."

Pat acted on this suggestion, but reluctantly,

and closed the door after him with as near a slam as he dared.

Drawing a small tissue-wrapped package from his pocket Mr. Ballardy handed it to Gillian.

"Your jewels, I believe, Mistress Chloe."

This was it!

Twice Jeff attempted to speak before his voice was under control.

"I'd like you to know, sir," he managed at last, "that this—this Chloe idea was mine, from the beginning."

"Indeed? You surprise me. The prank was typical of a lower-school child, I should have thought."

This quelled Jeff for the moment, but it had an opposite effect on his sister.

"And *I'd* like you to know," she challenged, with suddenly flaming cheeks and chin held high, "that it was as much my idea as Jeff's. They—we—couldn't have done it without me to play Chloe, which I did jolly well, too. You called me Chloe, you remember . . ."

"My dear young lady," Mr. Ballardy broke in quietly, "I'm quite ready to admit that you played the part convincingly, if youthfully. So convincingly that, for a moment perhaps, I was taken in. As you say, I called you Chloe—but, alas, ghosts have seldom, if ever, been known to leave tangible evidence of their manifestations behind them. I found the necklace the instant I snapped on my light . . . on the floor by the window. Incidentally, it's too valuable a piece for careless children to be playing games with. I think you must have—borrowed—it without your people's knowledge. You will return it—at once, please—to its proper and, I hope, secure place."

Jeff regained his voice. "You're dead wrong about the necklace, sir," he said, respectfully but firmly. "It's a fake, according to my grandmother."

They all breathed more easily. It was heartening, in their present chastened mood, to find Mr. Ballardy at fault about something.

In the silence that followed Jeff's statement, Mary Lee tried to make her confession also, but Mr. Ballardy ignored it. He had unwrapped the necklace and was pushing it around on the dark surface of the table with a gentle forefinger. He carried it to the window for better light. Finally he laid it on his white napkin, pulled a small magnifying glass from a pocket and examined it under that.

"Curious," he murmured at last, seemingly more to himself than to his interested audience, "I could swear that it's genuine. For years I've made a hobby of stones and settings and I can't help thinking that Mrs. Randall is mistaken in this instance. She doesn't know you borrowed it, of course, Gillian?"

"No. It was in the box-room with the costume—inside the wig."

"Inside a wig in a box-room," repeated Mr. Ballardy, shaking his head. "Well, I suppose it was safe enough there."

"It was safe enough on your table all night, too," Gill reminded him. "I only wore it for a few minutes, really . . ."

Jeff's next words were his undoing. "Perhaps it's as well you lost it before you went downstairs," he said.

His sister turned on him in a flash. "I did *not* go downstairs, Jeff Randall!"

"You did."

"I didn't! I didn't! I didn't!"

"Quiet!" ordered Mr. Ballardy in the voice that had, throughout his teaching career, silenced a roomful of boys. "Now . . . one at a time, please. What is all this, Jeffrey?"

Jeff launched into his story. While searching the corridor for the necklace he'd heard a slight sound and looked up to see Gill, in her long pale dress, at the top of the stairs. As he approached, she descended into the much lighter hall below.

"I couldn't think, sir, why she'd go down," he said. "But she did. There was moonlight from the little oriel window over the door and I could see her quite clearly. She looked up and laughed, and raised her hand. I naturally thought she wanted me to come along, so I went down, but she'd slipped into the dining-room. I searched the place over, but I never found her till I got back upstairs. She'd nipped up ahead of me, somehow, and was in bed! I dare say she thought it was funny to lead me a chase but I wasn't in any mood for jokes after crawling about looking for her beastly necklace. I ticked her off, and she had the nerve to deny the whole thing. She still denies it—and I don't like being lied to. That's all."

"And I don't like not being believed when I'm telling the truth," Gill said stubbornly.

She is telling the truth, too, Mary Lee thought. We all know she is, really. Who then—or what—had Jeff seen in the moonlight? Suddenly she caught her breath. The dog that had howled at midnight—she'd never believed it was Frolic! Nor had the girl on the stairs been Gillian!

"Jeff," she urged tensely, "Jeff—when—when—Gill—smiled at you, tell me—was it a sort of—come-hither smile?"

"Come-hither?" echoed Jeffrey.

"Provocative," translated Mr. Ballardy swiftly, excitedly. "An Americanism, perhaps, but very apt. Think, boy. What is your mind for!"

"Well, I came," Jeff admitted slowly. "I remember feeling as if I had to, rather. Gill looks quite unlike herself in that dress, you know—older, and as if she knew what she was about. You must have noticed it, Mary Lee."

But Mary Lee's eyes were raised to the portrait on the wall—the portrait of Chloe. The face so like Gillian's, the smile so different. . . .

And Mr. Ballardy was running long fingers through his grizzled hair.

"Dolt that I am!" he exclaimed. "There I remained secluded in my room, because I felt it would do a trio of young pranksters good to worry for a few hours—there I lay, snugly in bed, while Mistress Chloe—the ghost of Chloe—walked!"

They wondered, they pondered, and Mr. Ballardy asked innumerable questions.

Jeff apologised to his sister for doubting her word.

"But what about the luck Chloe's supposed to bring?" he asked. "She didn't give *me* any tips on the races. Oh, if this necklace turns out to be real, I suppose we'll have to believe she exchanged them, or something. But when?"

"Perhaps while the first one—Gran's necklace—was on Mr. Ballardy's table," suggested Gill wickedly. "*He* wouldn't have seen her, of course, even if he was awake, would he? But, if that's true, then a ghost *did* leave something real behind for once."

Mr. Ballardy looked nonplussed.

"My dear child," he said, "who knows? Certainly *I* can't explain it. But I shall ask your grandmother's permission to have the jewels examined at once. I shall take the necklace up to Town myself and if an expert pronounces it genuine——" Here he paused to rub his hands together with satisfaction. "I feel that we shall have near-proof of a most interesting manifestation. There's material for an article in this, though I must depend a great deal on you,

Jeffrey. You must do your utmost to remember . . ."

The door burst open and Pat breezed into the room.

"Your books have come, Mr. Ballardy," he announced. "Two big boxes. They're in the scullery. If you want to unpack them now, I could help you carry them upstairs. Shall I? And Gill, you're to bring the dishes out; your mother can't think why breakfast is taking so long."

Books?

The three young people exchanged glances.

"I arranged to have them sent while I was in London," Mr. Ballardy explained shortly. "I shall need them for some work I've undertaken to do down here."

"You mean, sir, that you'd already planned to stay on?" asked Jeff.

"Of course. And your grandmother very kindly agreed to the arrangement some time ago."

Again glances were exchanged—and rueful grins, as well.

"My word!" exclaimed Jeffrey. "In that case, the joke's on us. We put on this show, sir, simply to give you a new interest, because we thought you were bored to the point of leaving Somerhaze. Why—why—we need never have whistled up Chloe at all!"

15. *The Gymkhana*

MR. BALLARDY, it was agreed, could not have been nicer about the Chloe episode. He was especially gentle with Gill—Gill, who had been so nearly rude to him at breakfast time. He asked for—and got—half an hour with Jeffrey alone, during which he taxed the boy's memory for yet another description of the figure he had seen on the stairs.

"But the main thing is," Jeff said to Mary Lee soon after lunch, "that he's told Mum and Gran all about everything himself. He thought he'd better, and I couldn't have agreed more. Mum said her piece; we'd been discourteous to a guest, and so on. I was to apologise to Mr. B. and I did." Jeff broke off, grinning. "Shall I apologise to you, Mary Lee, for dragging you into all this? I've had plenty of practice lately. No? Well, I understand that Gran still thinks the necklace is a fake but she's agreed to let the old boy take it up to Town and have it examined—and she's sure I saw Chloe, just like my great-grandfather. Of course I *did*—unless Gill was walking in her sleep or something, poor kid. Mum's sent her upstairs to rest now and I'm off to the seven-acre field. The men are harvesting up there this afternoon."

Mary Lee thought she'd stroll down to the duck pond for a peaceful hour alone.

She never got there. Nor was the next hour a peaceful one.

Nearing Nannie's cottage she met her small brother, in tears.

"Pat!" she exclaimed. "What's the matter? Have you hurt yourself? Tell me."

"No-n-no," sobbed Pat, "It's—it's something awful! Mary Lee, I've—I've let Georgy out. He's loose!"

Pat had been left alone in Ivy Cottage while Nannie stepped down to the village for a few minutes. All summer he had been permitted to open Georgy's cage and allow the little green bird the freedom of the closed parlour. To-day he had not noticed that one of the windows was unlatched. A gust of air had done the rest. Georgy was, indeed, out. They could see him, still in the garden, but with the whole wide world to lure him on.

"And what will Nan do?" wailed Pat. "What'll she *do*, Mary Lee?"

"Hush, Pat," his sister soothed him. "Stop crying now—we'll get him back."

For half an hour they tried, and tried in vain. Georgy fluttered from bush to vine to apple tree, always out of reach. Sometimes he eyed them in a tantalising manner, cocked his head and chanted, "Georgy-Porgy—pretty bird—pretty bi-i-rd."

Mary Lee was growing desperate when she spied Ken crossing the yard. He had come down early from the seven-acre, to prepare for the milking. What was it Gillian had once said about Ken? "He has a magic way with animals." If only his magic might include birds!

A moment later Ken stood with them in front of the cottage. "Fetch the cage, Pat," he ordered. "And then you and your sister go indoors and stay there."

They watched from a curtained window as Ken sat himself down in the long grass, the opened cage beside him. He whistled, Georgy answered. "Pretty bird, pretty bird," crooned Ken—and Georgy flitted near. Ken never moved, even when Georgy came to rest on his shoulder, his hand. He continued to croon, but so softly now that they no longer heard words, merely the gentlest of sounds. Slowly, quietly Ken's hand moved towards the open door of the cage. Mary Lee held her breath—and the bird hopped inside as if he had no choice in the matter. Truly, this was magic!

Ken sat still for a moment beside the closed cage. Of course it was while he was carrying it to the cottage door that Nannie appeared on the scene.

"And maybe you'll tell me, young man, what's the meaning of this?" she suggested in an awful voice. "Though, I don't doubt, it'll take a deal of telling."

Pat did the telling; a joyful Pat filled with gratitude to Ken.

Nannie listened. Finally, nodding sagely, she said, "I'll just 'ot up the kettle—I left it simmering—and per'aps, Mr. 'awkins, you'll come in now and 'ave a nice cup of tea?"

It was well known that Ken had never crossed the threshold of Ivy Cottage before.

The little green bird chattered on. "Georgy Porgy—puddiny pie—Pretty Georgy, pretty bi-i-rd!"—just as if he had never brought about this astonishing state of things.

Mary Lee was tired of drama. And she longed to see her parents, in spite of the fact that, to borrow Nannie's phrase, she would have "a deal of telling to do" on their return.

In this respect she was lucky. They had prolonged their visit to Scotland by several days and—by coincidence—had travelled from London to Bridgwater on the train with Mr. Ballardy, who had been up to consult a jeweller about the necklace. He touched lightly on the subject of the children's prank, gave a detailed account of Jeff's encounter with the Somerhaze ghost, and added triumphantly that the necklace had just been pronounced genuine and of considerable value.

"Well," said Mrs. Randall, at supper that evening, "it's hard for me to believe, even now. Papa was so certain it was only a pretty fake. But, of course, after Jeff's encounter with Chloe anything is possible. And we're most grateful to you, Mr. Ballardy, for all the trouble you've taken on our behalf. I suppose we could always find a market for such a piece if actual catastrophe struck us but, at present, we're doing nicely and I wouldn't dream of selling it. Would you?"

"Not unless I had to," Mr. Ballardy agreed. "But I should insure it and place it in a bank for safekeeping. Fire, for instance, is always a hazard in the country."

"Oh, *no*!" protested Mrs. Randall vigorously. "It must be worn. Why, Rose has never had the necklace on."

"Nor ever will, I should think," Rose said, laughing. "Where would I wear such a thing, Mother? I live on a farm, remember. And, even among my old wedding clothes, I doubt there's a dress worthy of it."

But, just for a moment, her blue eyes looked wistful, and Mary Lee thought she'd like to see their pretty Rose dressed up.

Then her mother spoke. "You shall wear it!" she said. "At least you shall if I may borrow the house for a day. Do let me! I'll give a dinner-party! Just us and the Carys. they've been so kind this summer—taking us through the Court, giving us tea, having the children over for tennis. Don't you think they might enjoy a party?"

Mrs. Randall showed enthusiasm at once. They would all enjoy a party—it would be quite like old times, she said.

"But you're not to do a thing," Mrs. Wade went on. "You're to be strictly guests. I can get help from the village, surely?"

"Oh, the village will rally to the last woman," Mrs. Randall assured her. "They'll love it as much as a wedding. Mrs. Tuckfield is the one to see first—she cooks like an angel."

Mrs. Wade began planning immediately.

"I'll phone Lady Cary to-morrow," she said, "and settle the date. A few days before we leave, I think—it will keep us from being too sad."

"Don't let's talk about it, Mom," Mary Lee begged. "Not until we have to—*please.*"

"But, darling, our sailing date's all settled . . ."

"Don't tell me! Don't tell me!" protested her daughter, and sprang up from the table to help Gill with the dishes.

Her mother smiled, shrugged her shoulders and returned to the subject of her party.

Gillian had been in low spirits ever since the night she played Chloe. Though she rode in two shows and did well in both, she spoke of it without enthusiasm.

Mary Lee wondered if she was still troubled over the quarrel with her brother. Jeff didn't think so. "Gill's got a temper," he admitted, "but I've never known her to nurse a grudge."

It was not until two days before the Wiveliscombe Gymkhana that they discovered the cause of Gill's depression.

During lunch the telephone rang and she went to answer it. She pranced back to the dining-room an obviously happy girl.

"Susan Waring's got the measles," she announced gaily.

"Well, Gillian," protested her astonished mother, "is that any reason for you to gloat?"

"Oh, Mummy! She's got it lightly, they think. And I'm not gloating over Sue's measles, poor lamb. It's because Mary Lee can ride in the gymkhana! Jane talked to me; she's quarantined, of course, and she said we might as well have one of the ponies. I chose Skittles—he's the fastest... Mary Lee looked so out of things, sitting on the gate watching us; it's had me down for ages."

"You might have told us what was the matter," said Jeffrey. "I'd begun to suspect you of measles or something equally awful yourself."

Mary Lee, too, was pleased, if a little apprehensive. She'd never practised for the gymkhana. Still, she'd watched the others almost daily, and it wasn't as if she hadn't ridden Skittles before.

Gill was off like a shot as soon as lunch was

over to fetch the pony back from the Warings' place.

"He's in prime condition," she called to Mary Lee the instant she saw her waiting at the paddock gate. "And Jane says he knows the routine backwards because she and Sue meant to ride in this show themselves. He went well for me in that Whitsun thing, you remember, and you've got this afternoon and to-morrow to practise. Oh, we are in luck! I shall love poor Sue always for getting the measles right now."

There was a feeling of suppressed excitement as they rode towards Wiveliscombe on the day of the show—Mary Lee, Gillian and the two little boys.

It was a typical English summer morning. Pale golden corn stood in stooks, against the rounded shapes of the Quantock Hills—those waiting hills that changed from rose to lavender to deepest purple with the changing light.

The children walked their ponies down the final hill, selected a group of trees for shelter, replaced bridles with halters and removed saddles. They were to have a good rest before the show began. Gill had stabled them for the last few nights and much grooming had taken place.

"That mare," she said, seating herself on the grass and giving Colleen a frowning glance, "does kick sometimes, but if the junior jumping is scheduled early, it'll take the edge off her. You and I, Mary Lee, will concentrate on the relay race—we really ought to win it. And Pat and Toad should be even better for the under-thirteens."

The rest of the Somerhaze contingent arrived with lunch baskets by one o'clock. Rose had borrowed Mr. Chilcott's big car in order to accommodate them all, and it was followed, to everyone's surprise, by Mr. Ballardy in his own small rattling two-seater.

"*I* knew he was coming," Pat announced. "He wants to see me win the potato race."

Gill turned on him.

"Don't be too cocky, Pat," she ordered crisply. "There are some really good little riders out to-day. And, above everything, you aren't to show you mind when you lose. You'd better not eat much now, either—it slows you up."

Pat hastily returned a sandwich to the basket, and Toad followed his example.

But neither boy won the potato race. Nor did Gillian nor Mary Lee in their own class. It was won by Mary Ann Lambert on Badger.

"And Badger's not much bigger than Tuppence, either," said Mary Lee afterwards, glancing at the handsome little Exmoor with thick neck and well-shaped, intelligent head.

"Yes, he's a little bit of a thing, but fast! You look out for that pair in the Relay," Gill warned. "They'll nip right under your nose on the curves."

Mary Lee was very serious when she brought Skittles into line for this event. She meant to do her best for Gillian now. Clear round the field she must gallop, jumping one small obstacle which was no more than a row of straw bales (comforting thought) and hand the stick to Gill, who would be waiting on Colleen to receive it and finish the race.

Skittles was dancing with impatience.

As the starter shouted " Go," he leapt forward. They were round the first curve and into the straight with the hay-jump in sight and no one had passed them yet! But never would Mary Lee confess to Gillian how she raced to her share of that glorious victory. It was sheer terror of the thundering hoofs behind that drove her on. Surely they'd go over her and Skittles like the waves of the sea if they ever caught up! She glimpsed a golden streak that must be hay. Skittles had taken the jump in his stride when a small brown pony, his rider's long braids streaming like comets' tails, drew even with them. Mary Ann and Badger! Round the end of the field, down the other side the two ponies raced neck and neck. Mary Lee forgot the threatening hoofs that followed and thought only of out-running Badger. She could see Gill waiting, trying to keep Colleen under control. The Connemara mare was on her hind legs as Mary Lee thrust the stick into Gill's outstretched hand and plunged forward with a leap that she sincerely hoped Skittles would never try to imitate. When she had pulled him to a stop there was nothing to do but sit and watch Gill and Colleen romp round the course to win the race by lengths.

Gillian beamed on Mary Ann Lambert as the contestants all trouped out of the enclosure together.

"Tough luck," she said. "Your second relay let you down a bit, didn't he? I think Badger had Skittles beaten by a nose when you got to us."

"I was too busy to notice," Mary Ann answered. "But your mare certainly left the next bunch behind."

Gill and Mary Lee trotted back into the centre of the ring to receive blue ribbons, and it was announced through the loudspeaker that the event had been won by "Major Adcock's Colleen, ridden by Gillian Randall, and Susan Waring's Skittles, ridden by Mary Lee Wade—a young visitor from Virginia."

Jeff was waiting for them when they left the field the second time.

"Jolly good teamwork, girls!" he said, taking their ponies.

Gill decided to scratch the musical poles because she wanted Colleen to have a breather before the jumping competition, but Mary Lee had a try at it and managed to stay in until there remained only four riders, when she was beaten to her pole by a boy on a bobtailed little cob, riding bareback.

The junior open jumping was quite a different

matter from the other classes. This was serious, and the audience, which included a number of good adult horsemen, watched it with a critical eye.

Gill won it! After a second jump-off, too!

Mary Lee had never seen Jeff so pleased over anything as he was when his sister led the little procession of four to the middle of the enclosure to have the rosettes fastened on their bridles.

"Oh, but Colleen went beautifully for me," Gill said, patting the pony's lathered neck. "The first jump-off had me just a little worried because that boy on the bay is very clever over jumps, but the second was against the clock and Colleen's much faster than his pony."

After their picnic tea, Pat justified Mr. Ballardy's drive to Wiveliscombe. Gill had entered him, and Toad, in the obstacle race.

"Not that I expect much to come of it," she said, "because I didn't make them practise that sort of business, but they might as well take a last chance at something."

She explained the procedure to them carefully, as the starter did also a few minutes later. Half-way round the course lay a number of car tyres, on the other side the same number of canvas bags stuffed with straw: the small jump was somewhere between.

At this point Mary Lee sauntered over to the field, where Jeffrey joined her and they took up a good position by the enclosing rope. Here they watched the children line their ponies up for the start.

From the word "Go!" it was Pat's race. Tuppence launched himself like a small thunderbolt and fled round the turn, Pat hurling himself off and squirming through one of the tyres with the agility of an eel. Over the bales they were well ahead of the field. Pat was on the ground running beside his pony when the canvas bags were reached. Grabbing one, he flung it and himself across Tuppence's back and they were off, Pat's feet kicking wildly as he attempted to get a leg across the saddle. The onlookers roared with laughter, but he had succeeded by the time he met the straw jump on the second lap, and he galloped down the straight an easy winner.

Pat and Tuppence had caught the imagination of the audience, and the laughter turned to handclapping and cheers as the victory was unnecessarily announced through the loudspeaker.

"All the same," Gill said, recovering from her amusement, "it showed up his riding to advantage. He had complete control of his pony and he took that jump the second time without stirrups. He'd have done better bareback."

"He couldn't have done better!" Jeff exclaimed. "I never saw anything so funny in my life. And did you see Toad? He got through the tyre all right, but when he started to mount, Judy began backing and hauled him half-way across the field with her. Oh, golly! I haven't laughed so much in years."

Shadows lay long across the grass as the Somerhaze party assembled. Pat was hilariously excited and it was decided he'd best return to the farm in the car.

"You too, Mary Lee, if you like," Jeff said. "I'll ride Skittles home and Gill and I can take turns leading Tuppence. We'll be late, so keep some supper for us."

Pat had been asleep for hours and Mary Lee was in bed when Gill tapped on the door and entered her little room.

"Ken is looking after the ponies for us, bless him," she said. "I've brought you fifteen shillings—your half of the relay prize. I won four pounds on the junior jumping! It'll go towards a new saddle; my old one's getting awfully worn. Wonderful, isn't it?"

And Gillian spun away on her tired toes, towards a hot bath and her warm bed.

16. Dinner Party

MRS. WADE had gone ahead with arrangements for her dinner party, and when the day arrived, all was well in hand.

Mrs. Tuckfield took over the kitchen early and had brought with her a wide-eyed young niece to do the washing up and make herself generally useful. Mrs. Tuckfield's efforts were centred on higher things. A perfect trifle was, even now, chilling in the "fridge."

Mrs. Buffin was present also, having changed

her day for the " roughs " in order to miss none of the excitement.

Ruby Sweeting was coming in the evening to act as waitress, and word had gone round the village that "there 'adn't been such goings on at Zomer'aze—not since before the war, there 'adn't."

In only one respect had Mrs. Wade's plans gone astray; the Randalls were all as busy as bees.

"But why," asked Mrs. Randall, "should the village women have all the fun? Oh, don't think they aren't enjoying it. Nannie's in the kitchen now giving unasked-for advice. This party will be the talk of the Women's Institute for months to come."

She was unfolding a beautiful old creamy damask tablecloth as she spoke.

Rose polished silver in the scullery.

Gillian arranged the flowers. She had a gift for it, Mary Lee thought, eyeing the great cluster of white Japanese anemones against the dark oak panelling of the hall. Asters, in every shade of pink, mauve and purple, adorned the sitting-room, and she'd saved the few roses for the dinner table.

At eleven o'clock Mrs. Tuckfield brought in a tray with coffee for the adults and milk for the girls. The male members of the household had absented themselves for the day. Mr. Wade and Mr. Ballardy were visiting a museum in Bridgwater, Jeff and Pat were out with the harvesters.

"Jeff couldn't have done anything more helpful," Mrs. Wade said. "Pat would be dreadfully underfoot here, and he's so happy about lunching in the field with the men. But he must rest after tea."

Pat was to stay up for dinner.

His mother had, from the first, been torn between her desire for a formal party "just like one in an English novel," in which she knew children would never be included, and a longing to have Pat and Mary Lee present at an affair which she hoped they would always remember.

It was Rose who suggested the happy compromise of a children's table for four at one end of the long dining-room.

"Compromise is the order of the day everywhere now," she said gaily. "With three from the Court we'll be even numbers, and you can have your storybook formality at the big table. I'd like it, too, since I'm to wear the necklace for the first—and possibly only—time."

Mary Lee did some hasty counting on her fingers. "Three from the Court"—Sir Christopher, Lady Cary, Dick. Dick would, naturally, be a grown-up to-night, but he might not wholly ignore the children's table. She would wear her flowered silk, longer than most of her dresses, and becoming, she knew. A light dusting of powder would conceal the tiny freckles on her nose and she'd spend plenty of time on her hair.

A little before seven o'clock she presented herself at the door of her parents' room for inspection.

Her mother gave her her full attention for a moment.

"Take off the charm bracelet, dear," she advised, "that flowery dress is better without it—and over here, they prefer simplicity to anything else for young girls, you know."

"Gill's wearing a locket—a little heart-shaped one on a blue ribbon . . ."

"But with that plain white piqué, I suppose?"

"Yes. And she's brushed her hair *up*, Mom. It's like an angel's halo, but she still looks years younger than me."

"'Than I,' darling," corrected her mother. "Well, Gill's English and you're American—as typically so as the day you stepped off the ship. It's Pat who's changed. Run in and see if he needs any help with his tie, will you, daughter?"

Mary Lee thought of these words as she gave a final tug to her brother's tie. It was true. Pat, in flannel shorts, knee-length socks and a dark blue jacket, his hair a soft thatch on his round little head, and rosy colour in his once-pale cheeks, would be taken for an English boy anywhere. She had grown to love this country dearly; Pat belonged to it.

Days were growing shorter again; evenings chilly.

The sitting-room was at its charming best, with firelight and lamplight and flowers, though the curtains were not yet drawn when the party assembled there at a quarter-past seven.

Rosemary entered the room last of all, breathless from hurried dressing—and conversation stopped. Was this their hard-working Rose, usually to be seen in crisp cotton prints around the kitchen and dairy, tweeds in the garden or driving the shabby old car? Now she wore a cloudy grey dress that fell in soft lines to her slippered feet her chestnut hair was simply arranged, but round her throat, glittering and sparkling, catching every changing light, was Chloe's necklace.

Mrs. Wade broke the admiring silence.

"I suppose," she said, "that every man in the room is wondering if he'll be the lucky one to take you in to dinner."

Rose laughed.

"It's the necklace," she said. "The dress is so old, it's patched in places, but the necklace makes me feel as if I've stepped straight out of a fairy tale."

Of course it was Dick who took her in, who sat beside her at table, who paid her compliments until she blushed like a girl at her first party.

But, with the sweet on the table, he deserted the grown-ups and joined the children, ousting Pat for the purpose.

"Time he was in bed anyway," Dick said. "Rose and my grandmother were talking horticulture right across me as if I wasn't there. Such manners! Mary Lee must soothe my ruffled temper —I've heard that Southern girls are good at it

—and little Gillian shall tell me about her success at Wiveliscombe."

"Which one?" asked Gillian, on her guard as usual with her cousin. "Mary Lee and I won the relay, you know."

"Well done, girls! Congratulations to both of you," Dick said. "But I was thinking of the jumping competition, Gill. I heard—never mind how—that the Connemara went well and that you handled her perfectly."

This, then, was what lay behind Dick's flattering attention to the children's table, Mary Lee thought ruefully. There'd be serious horse talk as long as they remained in the dining-room. Turning to Jeff, she introduced the subject of cows, with all the animation of which she was capable.

But she couldn't wholly close her ears to the conversation between the other two, try as she would, and all interest in the relative merits of Jerseys and Ayrshires left her mind when she heard Gill exclaim, "Oh, Dick, you angel! You wouldn't!"

"I would," Dick said. "Of course the Major should do it himself but I'll jolly well see that he pays the entry fee anyway."

And now Gill couldn't wait to tell her great news.

"Mary Lee! Jeff!" she babbled. "Just listen! Dick's riding Jester in the Dunster Show and he's offered to send Colleen over in the horse van with him. I never dreamed of showing her there because it's much too far to ride and a van costs a fortune. She might have gone with Diana, but . . ."

"No, she mightn't," Jeff hastened to say. "I wouldn't risk poor Di getting kicked the very day of the show. Anyway, I arranged ages ago for her transportation with Mr. Chilcott's cattle."

Here was Dick's opportunity.

"Oh, does the pony kick?" he asked, all innocence. "That raises a question, doesn't it? Should I risk poor Jester's ribs, I wonder?" And he shook his head sadly.

But he hadn't the heart to tease Gillian for long when he saw her downcast face.

Gill vowed that Jester should enter the van first, that she herself should lead the pony in, that she would remain at her head to soothe and pacify every mile of the journey.

"Well, what you'd better do now," Dick told her, tiring of her eager promises, "is talk to your mother about it. I don't suppose she'll make any objections; she should be in an agreeable mood after the way I buttered her up all through dinner (which she richly deserved for looking the way she does this evening), but one never knows. Mothers take queer notions. And you've never ridden at Dunster before, have you?"

With all her happy excitement, Gillian's manners never deserted her. She said nothing to her mother until an opportunity offered in the sitting-room sometime later. Rosemary agreed, of course, pleased that Dick was making it possible for her daughter to ride in a really first-class show.

"We'll all drive over," she said, "and make a day of it. We must see how our Diana rates with the other Jerseys anyway."

"Just when is the Dunster affair?" Mrs. Wade asked. "We sail on the seventh, you know, and Warren thinks we should allow a week for London. Poor little Pat saw nothing of it when we were there in April, and I really must do some shopping."

"But Mom," Mary Lee protested, "the show's on the *third*!"

"And our rooms at the hotel are booked from the first." Then, seeing the stricken look on her daughter's face, Mrs. Wade added, "We'll all hate to miss the show, dear, but you'd have been less disappointed now if you had let me talk about dates when I wanted to. You wouldn't listen, you remember."

This was true; Mary Lee admitted it. But how *could* her parents have overlooked the importance of the Dunster Agricultural Show! Why Jeff had told them about it way back in the spring and they'd talked of the Jersey's chances there at intervals all summer. Jeff would be showing the cow himself. And now Gill was to ride at Dunster. Dick, too. What had London to offer compared with this?

"Mom," she said, in a very small voice, "couldn't you do your shopping in Bridgwater?

And I don't think Pat cares so much about London . . ."

But her mother had begun talking to Sir Christopher. One mustn't interrupt.

Pat had been sent up to bed some time ago, Jeff had melted from the room and Gill was already saying polite good nights. None of them understood.

Mary Lee, too, said good night—she even tried to smile, but she went upstairs with a very heavy heart.

Leaning in her little window, she gazed at the stars. Somewhere, an owl hooted—a lonely sound.

Gill came into her room without knocking.

"I'm not crying," Mary Lee told her, making a quick dab at her eyes.

"Of course not; it doesn't do any good," said Gill. "But I'll tell you how it is, Mary Lee. I'm not sure I even want to ride Colleen at Dunster, if you can't be there."

Mary Lee's aching heart was faintly comforted to know that Gillian cared as much as that.

Next morning everyone breakfasted in the dining-room because Mrs. Tuckfield, saying that she'd not had time for a "proper tidying" last night, was once more in charge of the kitchen. Rose came in from the garden to announce that she'd had an inspiration.

Why, she asked, shouldn't Mary Lee remain at Somerhaze for a few days after her parents' departure, go to the Dunster Show with the Randalls and travel up to Town alone. Rose would see her on to the London Express at Taunton, and her father could meet her at Paddington.

They thrashed the matter out then and there while three pairs of eager young eyes gazed hopefully from Mrs. Wade's face to her husband's, and back again.

Mr. Wade was the first to weaken.

"After all," he said, "Mary Lee did see a lot of London in the spring, and I've shown her much of the West Country since then. One thing she has missed—a typical cathedral city. I had planned a day at Canterbury or Winchester for all of us."

This was the moment that Mr. Ballardy, silent until now, chose to tip the scales in the children's favour.

"Wells," he pointed out, "is not too long a drive from here. The Cathedral is smaller than some but unsurpassed for beauty, as is the Bishop's Palace and the little town itself. If you will permit it, I should enjoy taking your daughter there on a Sunday. We might have lunch at one of the old inns and attend Evensong. A service would do much to impress the place on her memory, I think."

"Oh, Mr. Ballardy!" was all Mary Lee could say before turning appealing eyes in her mother's direction.

Both her parents realised at once that it would

be a privilege for her to see a cathedral city in such company. And she was quite capable of the journey to London alone. Mary Lee's spirits soared like a rocket.

Pat was quite the opposite, for he cared nothing about seeing "that old London" and a great deal that he was missing the Dunster Agricultural. So Mary Lee played up all the interests and excitement awaiting him in the great city. At the end of her glowing account her brother turned to the subject of pigs.

"We," he said, "aren't showing any this year because Duchess is our best one and Buffin thinks she's due to farrow any day now. They've promised to name one of the piglets after me." This fact seemed to give him much satisfaction.

Mary Lee helped with the packing. While sorting her clothes—for most of her things were to go with the family luggage—she unearthed her blue diary. Mrs. Wade, entering her daughter's room an hour later, found her deep in literary composition.

"My dear!" she exclaimed, eyeing the wild assortment of clothing on bed, chairs and table. "You haven't done a thing! And I'm waiting to finish the big suitcase."

"But, Mom, I found my diary, and it's too awful! I haven't written a word in it—not since——" And she flipped back the pages—"Not since the garden fête in June!"

"Never mind," her mother said, gathering up

an armful of blouses. "That's what usually happens to diaries, I believe. And none of us," she added, pausing in the doorway, "none of us is ever going to forget this wonderful summer."

Of course the packing got done in time. The luggage was bundled into Mr. Chilcott's big car, which Rose had borrowed, remembering the limitations of the Biscuit Tin.

Pat, disappearing at the last minute, was retrieved from a final visit to the sties.

Good-byes were said, with many promises of letters to be exchanged. Hands waved from the moving car. They were off—through the farm gate, turning into the lane—gone.

For a moment Mary Lee felt very odd.

"How about coming along for a look at Diana?" It was Jeff's quiet voice beside her.

She turned towards him and immediately all the interests of Somerhaze claimed her attention.

17. *Dunster Show*

MARY LEE's first view of Wells Cathedral (carefully planned by Mr. Ballardy, though she never knew this) was from the Green, and it looked, she thought, like a huge and very dignified valentine, made of stone lace.

The day was a complete success, from lunch in the dining-room at the Star, where she felt practically grown up, to the last faint echo of bells as they drove away from the little town, after an Evensong that she would never forget. And Mr. Ballardy was a perfect companion, for he understood that it was quite as necessary to watch the swans pull a rope and ring for their tea in the moat round the Bishop's Palace as it was to wander through the Vicar's close or see the Chapter House. Before the service he took her to the Lady Chapel behind the High Altar. It was like a little woodland, with slender columns arching up as young trees do, except that here one saw jewelled windows through them, and at the east end, Mary with the Holy Child in her arms.

Mary Lee was rather silent on the long drive home.

As they turned into the village lane she said, "I can't wait, Mr. Ballardy, to put it all down in my diary."

"You keep a diary?" he asked.

"Well, I meant to—but . . ."

"I know. It lapses, and when you write, you can't limit yourself to one dated page. Don't try, my child. And give your own impression of to-day's experience; nothing out of that guide-book in your lap, mind; you can study that later, if you like."

Mary Lee thanked him for her lovely day. "And Wells," she added, "will always be my favourite cathedral."

"One's first often is," Mr. Ballardy told her. "I enjoyed seeing it again through your fresh young eyes."

This was the nicest compliment she'd ever had, Mary Lee thought.

The weather, on the morning of the Dunster

Show, was uncertain—grey skies and occasional showers.

Mrs. Randall prophesied a larger crowd than if it had been fine. The farmers would all be there because it was a poor day for harvesting.

This was true. Farmers of all ages, in rough tweed jackets and leggings or Wellington boots, macintoshes on their arms were congregated around the sheep-pens and cattle stalls by the time the Somerhaze party arrived.

Gill, of course, had gone over in the horse van. But Jeff, starting almost at dawn, had made the journey in Mr. Chilcott's big cattle truck.

Mary Lee raised her eyes first of all to Dunster Castle, high above the big flat field with its milling crowd of people, children, dogs, through which seemingly hundreds of riders were constantly threading their way. She had glimpsed it before, but only from a passing bus on the main road. It was remote, and as romantic as a castle in a fairy tale.

Then the show claimed her whole attention.

How could she tear herself away from the small ring where the little Exmoor mares "with foal at foot" were being judged? Such long-legged, charming creatures, those foals!

She hung over the sheep-pens, remembering her bottle-fed lambs. Little black-faced Dorset-Downs those were.

Then the cattle. Rows upon rows of cows—Jerseys, Guernseys, Red Polls, Devons, Friesians.

And huge puffing bulls with rings in their noses.

After exchanging an amazed glance with the largest Friesian bull, Mary Lee was glad to encounter Jeffrey giving his gentle Diana a final polish.

"Jerseys are being judged next," he told her, and she ran back to the ropes around the central ring.

Judging took a long time and one cow looked much like another to her. She knew Jeff had hoped for first prize but he looked very proud and happy, nonetheless, when he led Diana out second in line with a big red and white rosette on her halter.

"The heifer was competing with some of the best Jerseys in the country," his grandmother reminded him. "And you showed her nicely. Buffin couldn't have done better."

Jeff was now free until the great parade of all prize-winning stock in mid-afternoon so he and Mary Lee went in search of Gillian.

They caught a glimpse of her, very slim and attractive in her birthday jacket and jodhpurs, topped by a little black velvet cap, cantering Colleen over the outer field.

"There's Dick!" Mary Lee exclaimed.

"Yes. He's probably giving her some last-minute advice. Dick's very capable, but I rather wish he'd let Gill alone just now. She's nervous over this thing anyway."

Colleen was entered in two classes, the first

open to "ponies not exceeding 14:2 hands, suitable for, and to be ridden by, a child under sixteen," the second the junior jumping event.

She didn't do as well as she should have in either. When Gill showed her in hand in the first class, she kicked, and was soon eliminated.

"And what else would you expect," Gill asked afterwards, "when her heels just missed one of the judges? They don't like it, naturally."

In the junior jumping, Colleen took exception to an unfamiliar obstacle and refused it so abruptly that her rider went off over her shoulder. Racing the pony at it the second time, Gill got her over neatly, but she was troublesome throughout and they were barely in the ribbons at the end—fourth place.

"It's simply our unlucky day," Gill said when she rode out of the ring and was met by Dick and her brother, with Mary Lee trailing along. "I never dreamed the little beast would refuse, or I wouldn't have taken that toss, of course."

"The pony's young, my pet," Dick soothed her. "So's Jester, and I only hope he goes as well for me this afternoon."

For some reason Mary Lee found herself alone when Dick's class was called. She had not realised it was his class until she heard Jester's name announced as he trotted into the big enclosure, and then she would not hunt for Jeff and Gillian for fear of losing her place by the ropes.

What really awful-looking jumps, she thought,

as Dick circled the chestnut around and headed him at the first one. She didn't see how any horse could get over the two spread poles near where she was standing. But Jester, galloping easily, made nothing of them at all. He cleared the lot with no faults.

There were many contestants in this class and Mary Lee's excitement mounted as rider after rider entered and left the ring, very few with Dick's clean record. Surely there must be a jump-off. Two were called for, the second against time, with only three riders to compete. The first of these took down two poles, the next several bricks out of the wall.

As Dick and Jester cantered in to make their final effort, Mary Lee was breathless with excitement.

Jester sailed over the hedge, over the hurdle, the big farm gate, the wall, thundered down to the spread poles—the last jump of the course. He cocked his ears, took off well away from it and cleared it with apparent ease!

Mary Lee, wriggling her way through the crowd, started running for the little assembling ring where Dick would be. Suddenly she turned shy. Gill and Jeff would meet him there and that was all right, but he had grown-up friends among the other riders; she had seen them talking and laughing together before lunch. So she altered her course and brought up at the Biscuit Tin, from which vantage point she watched, with

Mrs. Randall and Rose, while the blue ribbon was pinned on Jester's bridle.

"A splendid performance, wasn't it?" Mrs. Randall was in high spirits. "Dear Madge should have been here to see Dick ride."

After the Parade of Prize Animals—horses and cattle—in which Jeff, once more, led his beloved Diana, there was a quiet interval for tea.

"And do I need it!" said Dick, coming up with Jeff on one side and Gillian, full of excitement over her cousin's success, on the other.

Everyone congratulated him and he beamed on them.

"Yes, I'm pleased with that young horse," he acknowledged. "Gill is disappointed, I think, because he's not entered for the open, but I know he's had enough for one day. I'm starting him home very soon. But first—one more cup of tea, one more rock cake and I'll be in a mood to grant anyone's wishes. What shall it be, girls? I see a stand just over there selling repulsive little objects. Shall I buy you a fairing? Speak up Mary Lee—now's your chance."

He smiled at her, and before Mary Lee could stop herself, it was out.

"Oh, Dick," she begged. "Oh, Dick. Could I come to tea at your gazebo? To-morrow? To-morrow's my very last day, you know."

"Do you really want to?" he asked.

Was he annoyed by her silly request? But he was waiting for an answer.

"I've wanted to all summer," she confessed.

"And so you shall," he promised, getting up. "I'll phone in the morning about time and things. . . . Are you coming with me in the van, Gillyflower? Drive home with your mother if you're tired. I'll protect Jester from your wretched little kicking Colleen."

But Gill would not hear of it and went off with her cousin, hotly defending the Connemara pony.

Since Buffin was quite capable of receiving and unloading Diana, Jeff decided he'd take the vacant seat in the car and Rose thought they should be starting. But Mrs. Randall begged to wait and see the hounds—the West Somerset Pack, which would be parading in a few minutes.

Even as she spoke, a horn sounded, heads turned.

Across the green turf came the hounds, flowing like a dappled moving sea around the Master's big horse. As if to welcome them, the sun sent a shaft through the grey clouds, brightening the pink coats of Master and Huntsman, striking a spark of light from the Master's horn.

Mrs. Randall was out of the car in a flash, standing on tiptoe, her eyes shining.

"Oh, the beauties!" she murmured. "The lovely, lovely things!"

The hounds turned in and circled the enclosure to a round of applause—first at a trot, then at a canter. The Master sent them forward, always together—and the applause doubled.

Mary Lee was breathing fast, her heart thudding. But the picture that pleased her most was when the hounds trotted quietly from the upper end of the ring, where the little brooding castle looked down on the pack from its tree-clad hill, and the riders, ready for the next event, sat like statues on their horses watching them pass.

"And that will slow us up on the road home," Rose announced. "Oh, but it was worth waiting for, wasn't it, Mother?"

"I used to walk hound puppies each year," Mrs. Randall said dreamily, as the Biscuit Tin left the show grounds. "The Master always gave us a little silver spoon with the puppy's name on it to show his appreciation. There are seven or eight of mine left, I believe." She turned in the front seat and looked at Mary Lee, who was sitting with Jeff in the back of the car. "You enjoyed seeing the pack, didn't you, child?"

"I loved it," Mary Lee said simply. "More than anything at the show, I think."

"Gill must have six of those spoons, someday," Mrs. Randall went on. "But you shall have the seventh, Mary Lee. I want to give you some little thing from the farm to remind you of your Somerhaze summer."

"Oh, Mrs. Randall, as if I could ever forget!" Mary Lee protested. "But, if you really mean it, I'll take the greatest care of my spoon and keep it all my life."

She was enchanted with the names on the spoons when Mrs. Randall brought them out.

"Valorous," "Vanity," "Wistful," "Wanderer," "Tumult," "Trumpeter" and "Sorrowful."

"Oh, hounds have beautiful names," her hostess agreed. "All the puppies from one litter must be given names commencing with the same letter, and I usually walked a couple, so my spoons are in pairs. Which will you choose, dear?"

Mary Lee selected "Sorrowful" because she thought Gill's spoons should remain in pairs.

No words could express her thanks. On impulse, spoon in hand, she threw her arms around Mrs. Randall and kissed her cheek.

Next morning Mary Lee packed her small suitcase, wondering all the while if Dick would remember about tea in the gazebo. Would she hear the phone if it rang? Would it be answered promptly enough? Would someone remember to tell her if a message came?

At eleven-thirty Gill asked if she didn't want to pay a last visit to the ponies. There was nothing to do but go, and of course it was while she was down at the paddock that Dick called. Rose told her about it at lunch.

"He's asked Mr. Ballardy, too," Rose said. "So he will take you over at four o'clock."

And that, Mary Lee thought, was very nice. Mr. Ballardy would fit into the picture and she felt a little shy of a tea-party with Dick alone. Conversation must be kept up, and whatever would she find to talk about?

She had seen the outside of the gazebo several

times—a delightful little brick building with a pointed roof, perched above the high wall surrounding the Cary Court estate.

Mr. Ballardy left his car near the gatehouse and Dick met them as they strolled across the lawn.

The gazebo boasted two small rooms, one above the other, but Dick said the lower one housed only garden chairs and spiders as he led his guests up an outside staircase to a green door with a curved top and a narrow window on either side. Mary Lee wanted to squeal with delight when she stepped inside, but of course she didn't. What a place!

There was a single sash window with pale green curtains in each of the side walls, and opposite the door a graceful little white mantelpiece and a black iron grate where a kettle hissed cosily.

A tarnished looking-glass in a round gold frame hung above the mantel and the few pieces of furniture included a small tea-table, ready set with pretty china and a bowl of flowers.

"Oh, but what was it for?" she asked. "This sweet little house, I mean."

"It would have been called a Pleasure House," Mr. Ballardy told her. "And was built in the time when ladies had leisure to meet their friends here with no greater purpose than to watch the passers-by. The stagecoach was, I believe, the great excitement of the day."

Dick had filled the teapot and a Guernsey jug, and he asked Mary Lee if she would like to pour. She would, indeed, but she must do it with ease and grace. She remembered to ask about milk and sugar, she remembered to refill the pot from the jug, she remembered to offer second cups. It took concentration, and meanwhile Dick and Mr. Ballardy got off on the subject of Oxford. Would they forget that she was present?

Dick was a perfect host. He plied her with little pink-iced cakes. He said, "Next time you're over, Mary Lee, your mother must bring you up to see me at Oxford. In the spring term, mind. You shall stay at The Golden Cross and come to tea in my rooms and I'll take you on the river and to Addison's Walk to look at the deer."

"Oh, Dick!" breathed Mary Lee, her eyes wide. "Would you really? In three years, maybe? I'll be sixteen then."

"Exactly the right age for a girl to visit Oxford," approved Mr. Ballardy, rather surprisingly. "And one word of advice, Mary Lee—you must wear a charming, wide-brimmed leghorn hat, perhaps with a wreath of field flowers—certainly it must have long, black velvet ribbons . . . ."

Even Dick was overwhelmed by this.

"She's much more apt to come bareheaded, I should think, sir," he said. "A hat like that would be sure to blow off—on the river, anyway."

"They always did," mused Mr. Ballardy, "and floated slowly out of reach downstream. . . ."

Mary Lee and Dick exchanged glances, half-puzzled, half-amused.

Mr. Ballardy had, apparently, gone off in a daydream.

Dick shrugged a shoulder and turned to a small shelf in the corner of the room which held a few books.

"Um-m-m . . . what shocking taste I have," he commented. "Almost nothing here that's fit for you, my child . . . Wait, this will be just the thing, I think."

In his hand was a small, slender volume of Shakespeare's lyrics.

Mr. Ballardy, alert once more, offered his fountain pen, and Dick wrote on the fly-leaf, with a fine flourish, "Mary Lee Wade—a reminder for a date with Dick," and, down in one corner, "Don't forget the hat!"

Mary Lee said "Oh-o-o!" And then she thanked him very conventionally for the book, for the party, for showing her the gazebo. But all the time she was promising herself that she'd learn every one of Shakespeare's lyrics by heart!

Leaving Somerhaze next morning was hard. It would have been harder except that Mary Lee kept thinking of all she had to tell her parents. So much had happened since their departure—the Dunster Show, her tea-party at the gazebo, Wells. And she couldn't wait to show them Dick's book and her silver spoon with Sorrowful's name on it.

Everyone came out in the garden to see her off. Gillian gave her one cold, hasty kiss, then darted into the house, the spaniels at her heels.

Rosemary was waiting in the car and Mary Lee didn't quite know what to do.

"Will—will Gill be out again?" she asked Jeffrey.

"Shouldn't think so," he answered. "The poor kid's all upset—about your leaving, you know. She'd be worse if she wasn't going over to the Court almost at once to ride that young horse of Dick's."

"She is! But I thought Dick wouldn't ever let her!"

"No more he would," Jeff said, grinning. "But it's what she asked for when Dick—most foolishly—told you girls you could have whatever you wanted. Gill got a promise out of him on the way home in the van."

At the delicious idea of Gill's outwitting her cousin, Mary Lee had to laugh, which made it easier for her to climb into the Biscuit Tin beside Rose.

Jeff ran down ahead of them to open the gate. As they drove through he tossed a tiny package into Mary Lee's lap.

"From Gill and me both!" he called after her.

Mary Lee did not open it until her London train had left Taunton far behind. Under the layers of paper, in a newly polished if battered old silver frame, was a little picture of Somerhaze. Somerhaze—with white flowers just showing through the rusty iron garden gate, and flowering vines clambering up the sunny southern wall. Two small figures—a younger Jeff and Gillian—on two shaggy ponies, rode down the rough drive leading from the barns.

Mary Lee looked long at the small picture, and for many miles she watched the green English landscape slide by the window through a blur of tears.

But she would come back, she told herself, to England and to Somerhaze. The old house had stood so long, sheltering Randalls within its walls, that surely it, and they, would be waiting to welcome her whenever she returned.

THE END